The Viking Girl

The Viking Girl

by

William Power

The Pentland Press Ltd
Edinburgh·Cambridge·Durham

By the same author:

Devil's Delight (1989)

First published in 1993 by
The Pentland Press Ltd.
1 Hutton Close
South Church
Durham

ISBN 1 85821 047 X

Typeset by Spire Origination Ltd, Norwich
Printed and bound by Antony Rowe Ltd., Chippenham

Chapter 1

The rough road was barely more than a cart track. It was uneven and muddy, rain having fallen almost continuously for the past two days, but now the sun was shining through billowing clouds on a late September afternoon. The long column of men moved as quickly as possible, breastplated mounted spearmen at its head; behind them, without benefit of armour but with helmets of leather, were the bowmen and spearmen on foot with shields, then came the swordsmen. Bringing up the rear of the column was the King of Wessex, Ethelred the First, and his retinue. Finally came the horse-drawn carts carrying the army's essential supplies. There were more than three thousand men making their way towards Nottingham, now in the grip of the Danes, and they had been on the move for several hours from Medeshampsted in Mercia with the object of freeing the town from the Vikings.

The marching men, cheerful enough for most of the time since leaving Medeshampsted, were now footsore, their leather clothing and boots wet, their shields getting heavier by the minute.

The head of the army had reached high ground. Suddenly there was a shout from a leading horseman. He held his right hand up high and the column slowly halted. The King gestured to the aide mounted beside him and the man turned and spurred his horse. He reached the man poised on the ridge quickly and there immediately below them was the River Trent, vaguely reflecting sun in its dark, still waters. Beyond the river, away to the right, thatched buildings could be seen.

'That's Nottingham, sir. What are our orders?' asked Aldan, a Captain of cavalry, veteran of many battles fought in defence of his native Wessex and other kingdoms besieged by Vikings during the last twenty years.

Edwig, Earl of Bedford, scanned the other side of the river. He could see no sign of any people, the only evidence of any life was sheep and some cattle grazing contentedly in a field close to the bank on the other side of the river.

'Wait and tell the men to rest,' he told Aldan and rode back to the King.

'Sire, we have reached the Trent and Nottingham is but little more than five miles away.'

'And the Dane?'

'None that can be seen.'

There was a momentary silence.

'Then they must be safely entrenched in the town.' The King's voice showed some concern and not a little irritation. He turned his horse and looked around him. To his left, about a quarter of a mile away, was a small wood. Though it would not give all his men cover, he thought it a suitable place to stay for a short spell. He had moved quickly on getting a plea for help from his brother-in-law Burgred, King of Mercia, after the sack of Nottingham by their mutual enemy, and was well satisfied with his progress so far. He could now plan his final moves. Beyond that Ethelred would give no more thought, being a man with no great liking for war and simply wanting to do only that which his kingly and brotherly duty demanded. He turned back to the Earl having made his decision.

'Very well, Edwig, we shall camp here until our plans are laid. See that the tent is prepared,' he told his aide and rode off.

The conclave of King and his advisers lasted some time. The King got increasingly annoyed when his plan for a quick frontal assault on Nottingham was opposed by all except Edwig. The King's wish was to waste as little time as possible, so as to get the battle over and done with very quickly. The three of his counsellors more experienced in military matters and more appreciative of the martial skills of the Danes — particularly their ability to defend as well as attack — advocated a more cautious approach. They wanted a preliminary probing of the Danish defences by a hundred bowmen, with spearmen in reserve, and cavalry only to be used in the final assault. Their view was that the enemy would be well prepared for the more obvious line of approach from the west of the town which had some sort of roadway, though primitive.

CHAPTER ONE

The King finally brought the meeting to an end by declaring that his force would cross the Trent at the place where they were presently camped, then go on to the town. But he did accept a suggestion by Sir Olfrith that the crossing be made initially by the bowmen, before first light, so that the element of surprise would be the greatest. Ethelred then settled down on a makeshift bed to get a few hours' rest. The others then left him and went to prepare their men for the morning.

After Edwig had given his men their orders a group of them had gathered under a tree.

'So we 'as to fight, I say us 'as to get something more than stale bread to eat,' said Black Edward, a man of some six and a half feet tall, with long black hair down to his shoulders and a beard which covered his massive chest. He drew the longest bow in the whole of Wessex — an area extending beyond Exeter in the West to the coast beyond London in the East — and had been known to hit a man or animal at a distance of almost two hundred yards.

'We might get some hare,' suggested Harald, a blonde youth standing close by.

'I was thinking sheep or goat,' snapped Black Edward. The big man collected his bow and arrows from the ground in front of him. He turned and made his way out of the wood without glancing right or left, expecting the half-dozen or so to follow.

An hour's hunt proved to be successful. A lamb had strayed from its mother with a small flock on the other side of the field and was grazing peacefully when an arrow from the big archer's bow pierced its neck. It was bundled into a sack and the men were making their way back to the camp when one of them, walking close to a hedge, put his hand up for the others to stop. There was a faint rustling noise, then it stopped. Silence for a few moments, then the sound started again. They followed it until a dark figure appeared at a gap in the hedgerow. It was quickly seized upon by two men who pulled it out into the open. It was a man, raggedly dressed, with matted hair and dark, staring eyes. He fell to his knees and looked wildly round him, babbling something which they could not understand.

'It's a Danish look-out, come to find our camp,' called out one of the men who had seized the pathetic figure.

'That can't be so — the man can't talk,' said the blonde youth. 'Let's take him back.'

After some talk, in which the suggestion was opposed by Black Edward because he had not thought of it, there was general agreement that the man be taken back.

Approaching the camp they met a horseman, Athyll of York, an Officer of cavalry who had been forced south with the onset of the Danish invasion of Northumbria. He had been making a final round of the sentries and ensuring the security of the camp.

He drew his sword as the small group of men came close to him and called the usual challenge.

'We are some of Edwig of Bowood's men, sir,' called back Harald, his grip like a steel band on the arm of the unfortunate shaking creature they had caught. Black Edward quickly passed his bag to the man behind him but Athyll had brought his horse closer and had seen the move.

'Well, Bowood's men. Did he give you permission to leave?' he asked.

'No, sir.' Harald's reply was brief and unapologetic.

'We wus hungry, sir, and looking for some food as us are to battle in the morning,' put in Black Edward surlily.

'And I see you were successful — what is in the bag?' There was silence and Athyll repeated the question, more sternly now.

'A couple of hares, that's all,' put in one man, hoping this would be accepted and the matter passed over.

'Give me the bag,' ordered Athyll and inside found the bloody remains of the lamb. He threw the bag back into the group where it was expertly caught by young Harald.

'Right, you may keep the animal since it is not one of the royal fawn — had it been so the trees yonder would have had your bodies hanging from them by the morning.' He dismounted and faced them, a tall man, clean shaven, with long reddish-brown hair. Though he wore his helmet he had divested himself of his coat of mail.

'You have a man captive there. You . . .' pointing to the big bowman, 'tell me, who is he?'

Black Edward stepped forward, smirking with self-importance. The rest of the men stood glumly waiting as the man was pushed toward Athyll. They did not like the handsome Northerner who had a reputation as a strict disciplinarian and who had a short, sharp way with traitors and cowards as well as dealing ruthlessly with the Dane. The men were wondering how they were going to be dealt with for breaking camp and hoped the capture of a possible spy for the enemy would get them praise rather than censure for the misdemeanour.

'We found the man a few yards back, sir,' lied Edward. 'We think he wus trying to get to the camp.'

Athyll was closely examining the man's face. There was an unintelligible noise coming from the man and he was desperately trying to say something. Though the cavalryman listened carefully he could make no sense of it. Then he bent forward and gently opened the man's mouth as he recalled a similar sight he had seen in a village near York after the Danes had left a trail of devastation and misery in their wake.

The man had no tongue. Athyll closed the mouth and examined the man's clothing. He turned back to the men. 'This man is no servant of the Dane but a victim. His tongue has been cut out.'

Athyll mounted his horse. 'Take him to the camp and give him some food. He will have to wait until we take Nottingham for some clean clothing.' He rode off to make one last tour of the camp.

The little group watched him go, then turned to their charge. He seemed quieter now and as they moved off he followed obediently. It was too late to light fires; their smoke and flame would have been seen for a great distance. Black Edward stripped the animal and cut up rough pieces for his companions to eat raw. But he resolutely refused to give the dumb man any, saying that it was only for those who would have to face the Danish army. Young Harald protested but was overruled by the rest. The man was given some stale bits of loaf and Harald did manage to slip him a small piece of meat on a bone which he wolfed hungrily, not having fed properly for several days; only berries and a couple of voles.

It was cold now and a thick mist had risen, covering the encampment in a haze so that one person could hardly distinguish another. But three or four of the bowmen watched the stranger with amazement as he took out a small metal tool from inside his ragged jacket and began to dig earth a foot in depth. Then settling himself in the crude opening he pulled leaves on top of him until only part of his head and an ear were visible. Two of those watching thought it a good idea and were thankful when they woke feeling quite warm and refreshed, their rough bed having proved more comfortable than the hard cold earth.

Before the cold light of dawn had appeared some fifty bowmen had made their way along the bank of the river to find a suitable crossing place. They eventually came to a small footbridge to the east of the town. They were ordered to cross by Edwig Bowood, he following, leaving a further fifty men awaiting their move. Behind them came the spearmen and, hidden in reserve in the wood, were the mounted men including the King and his guard.

The first soldiers crossed safely and moved forward cautiously, making use of every bit of cover. There was no sign of the Dane and everywhere was as quiet as the grave. As the first of the archers slowly made their way toward the town the second group crossed, still keeping some distance between themselves and the leading men. Athyll, the sole horseman watching the progress of the second wave — the first now being out of sight — from the ridge of high ground to the West, could see that progress was being made without any opposition; in fact the first group had reached the town. Greatly pleased, Athyll rode back to report to the King.

Ethelred was puzzled by the news which was not what he had expected. However, it was too late to change any plans and he was reminded by Sir Olfrith that the enemy had probably prepared a surprise and was simply biding time before making any moves. This pessimistic view was not entirely shared by the others close to the King. He now gave the order to move forward, somewhat encouraged by the notion that he might possibly have the larger force and be able to evict the Danes from the town without too much trouble.

As the cavalry proceeded slowly to ford the river, Bowood and his men had reached the outskirts of Nottingham. He ordered them to halt and they instantly sought what shelter they could find. They stayed like this for some time but there was no sign of movement. In fact, the first few simple thatched dwellings appeared to be deserted. Bowood was not content to wait for long, however. If there was going to be a battle the sooner it began the sooner it would be over.

Striding forward he led the way along the narrow street. The rest of his men soon followed, some cheering. This was taken up by the rest and was turned into earsplitting screams as long pent-up feelings were released. Oddly, there was still no sight of any Dane. A few heads appeared cautiously round the entrances to the small buildings made of a wooden framework covered with thick straw. But of the invader there was no sign.

The second group of archers had now entered the town and people were beginning to come into view from their houses. Some brave souls, recognising the Anglo-Saxon dress of the soldiers and hearing the welcome cries in familiar accents, came out into the street, first to gape in amazement, then to wave hesitatingly. Soon there were over five hundred men in the town having entered from the East. The rest had been ordered to wait on the outskirts. The cavalry had crossed the river by a more direct route and were to the south of the town. The shouting and cheering by his men had died down and the King was contemplating his next move when a man carrying a spear came running into the large group of horsemen. He was stopped by a sword being pressed to his chest. No-one was going to take any chances with the King's life at this stage of the encounter. The man appeared to be distressed but this was only from the effort of running as fast as he could with the news. He panted for breath while a cavalryman watched impatiently.

'Well, man, what is it? What have you to say?'

At last the man was able to get his breath. 'It's the Danes. They's gone from Nottingham, sir,' he gasped excitedly.

'The saints be praised. Can this be true?' cried the devout cavalry officer. Athyll came riding up to enquire what was happening.

'This man says that the Danes have left the town,' he was told.

'Do you know this for certain?' Athyll snapped.

''Tis word from John, the leading citizen who has told our Commander, sir,' replied the spearman resolutely, now fully recovered. Athyll, satisfied that he heard the truth, rode back to the King. Athyll could not get to him directly, surrounded as he was by his guards, but he spoke to the Earl of Bedford who passed on the good news to the King.

Later, at the head of his cavalry, the King entered Nottingham in triumph to the relief, though undemonstrative, of its citizens who had spent the winter suffering at the hands of the foreign invaders. There were sad sights of their vandalism: burnt-out houses and recently dead men still tied to posts where they had been murdered.

But to demands from Bedford and others that the Danes be pursued without delay, the King was adamant. There was nowhere between here and York where they could entrench themselves and he was not prepared to pursue them for that distance, particularly as they were reported to have been in Nottingham in some force. The reason why they had chosen to leave without a fight was a mystery but this fact did not detract from the pleasure of having got a bloodless victory. King Ethelred reined his horse outside the entrance to the homestead, which had the appearance of being the abode of the leading citizen. He was appalled at the sights that he had encountered since entering Nottingham and was determined to get a full account of the atrocities that had been committed.

He urged his mount forward into the large courtyard. To the right was a once-pagan temple which had been put to Christian use and had a small wooden cross on the roof above the doorway. Beside that was another small building which probably housed the servants; immediately in front was a timber-framed building which was the main hall. Placed behind this building was a stable and an outhouse used for the storage of oats and other domestic requirements.

As the King and his escort stopped at the main building a man carrying a cross in his right hand came out and went down on one knee, nervously babbling some sort of greeting.

'Get up, man, and fetch your master, whoever he is. Tell him King Ethelred is here.'

The man looked up in surprise at the men mounted in imposing array before him. Then, bowing to the central figure he thought to be the King from his demeanour and dress, he turned and ran so quickly into the building that he nearly collided with the person coming out. He was a tall, thin man, with sharp features and a straggly white beard. He was wearing a silk cloak, specially imported from France, fastened in the centre on the right shoulder and elaborately adorned with brooches inlaid with garnet and gold filigree work applied to the background.

The man bowed with extravagant fervour, then he looked up at the royal personage with pale blue eyes squinting short-sightedly.

'Welcome to my humble home, my lord. I am John, a merchant weaver of this town and at your service. What is your pleasure, sire?'

The man's high-pitched voice, almost a whine, grated on the King's ears who mentally noted that he would spend no longer than was necessary in the company of this person. However, he had had little rest the previous night and was tired. He also felt the need for a good meal for the first time in several days and thought this man could well afford to supply one. He dismounted and immediately two servants appeared and led his horse away. Without a word the king strode past the anxious merchant and found himself in a large hall, nearly a hundred feet long with a porch at one end which led into another room. The principal seat was placed in the centre of the north side of the hall; another seat, reserved for honoured guests, was placed opposite beneath a window. In the centre was a fire, burning low at this time as the merchant believed in conserving his fuel stocks.

CHAPTER ONE

After a quick meal of bread and fish from the Trent, John the merchant promised a full board in the evening and he called his wife and two daughters to get their instructions for the meal. The wife, Selia, was a short, plump woman, dressed in a brown under-tunic which touched the ground and had long, close sleeves with a round, close fastening at the neck. The blue overgown had a full, gored skirt, shorter than the undergarment; the sleeves were loose, with a decorative border. The headdress was a blue veil put over the head and crossed over a shoulder, and her shoes were made of soft brown leather.

The woman blushed as she entered the presence of the King. She quickly noted what was required of her and wanted to return to her own quarters immediately but the daughters stood transfixed on encountering the imposing company. Similarly dressed to their mother, they gaped at the royal party at the table — not a pretty sight as their looks could hardly be said to be of the most attractive kind, both girls being flat-chested and having features of an unhealthy yellow tinge.

At last Sir Olfrith could not contain his amusement at the sight and this roused the merchant to usher the women out of the room with some embarrassment and irritation.

After the servants had cleared the table the King invited their host to join the company and the questioning began. Firstly, Sir Galwain wanted to know when the Danes had left. The previous night just after dark, he was told, and they headed north. That meant they had a twenty-four-hour start on any pursuer, Galwain reminded the others. It appeared that the Danes had been using Nottingham for their temporary quarters and had other plans to execute in the coming spring and summer months. After giving some more information about the number of people in the town, their state of health, food supplies, and so on, the merchant was asked the most important question of all.

'Now, why were some citizens tied to posts and murdered?' asked Bedford quietly. John hesitated and nervously wiped his lips with the back of his hand.

'Come, man, answer the question,' ordered the King, who until now had been silent.

John took a breath. 'I know of only two who were treated in this way, sire, on my oath as a God-fearing man. They were men who had been caught stealing from the Danes and were impaled on the stake just as we ourselves would have dealt with them, my lord.'

'Reports that the King already has state that at least ten bodies have been found,' put in Bedford.

'I have no knowledge of that, sir, indeed I have told you all that I know,' the merchant replied primly, with an air of injury that his word had been doubted. There was a pause whilst the company considered him and the implications of what had been said. At last the King, wanting to rest, stood and faced the man whose eyes had now turned away from the others and were looking down at the stone floor.

'Send the Thane here so that arrangements can be made to prepare defences and restore what can be restored,' Ethelred told the man.

'But, my lord, that is not possible since Offren is dead and his body burned but two days before.' The words came out breathlessly as this was a reminder of another problem facing the people but notably himself as one of the leading citizens. The King was unperturbed by the news. 'Very well, I will appoint another Thane before I leave,' he said. John was plainly relieved at the promise and led the way out of the hall, protesting volubly that the King would have his own room whilst he was a guest, and that the King had only to make his wishes known for them to be granted.

That evening a meal was prepared that was indeed fit for a king. A whole pig had been roasted and served with locally grown vegetables: there was some fish and finally local fruit. The mead also flowed freely so that by the end of the meal only Sir Thomas was sober because all his life he had believed wine and ale to be a slow poison.

As the evening wore on the King demanded entertainment and the merchant hurriedly sent out for a singer who lived close by, and her accompanist on the lyre. This was much to the disgust of his daughters, both of whom thought their singing would have pleased the King. Hearing that the merchant wanted performers, a juggler also appeared to add his part to the proceedings. But although the singer was the best in the locality, she was far from being trained in her art and the juggler nothing like the real thing. Fortunately, the assembled company was not, by this time, in a position to be able to apply any critical faculties to what was being presented to them. So, by the end of the evening, when the performers had been paid and John's guests had taken to their beds, the merchant was the only dissatisfied person.

Early next morning the King prepared to return to his seat at Winchester. But before he left he appointed Edwig the new Thane and gave him the title of Knight. He also made a tour of the town, noting the damage by vandalism and other unpleasant marks of the Danish occupation, such as the desecration of the Church, and he ordered a hundred silver coins to be paid from the royal funds as payment towards the cost of the restoration that had to be made.

Leaving some thirty horsemen and as many archers under the command of Athyll to assist in restoring the place to normal, the King gathered another small force of cavalry to return to Winchester with him. The remainder of the men who had accompanied him on the expedition were disbanded and told to return to their homes. However, there was no order that they should not stay in the place and this is what several of them, having come from as far west as Glastonbury and Somerton, decided to do.

As the King left with his force on their journey south a few people gathered to see them on their way. These Mercians had experienced Danish occupation throughout the year; now the Saxons were here many were almost as fearful and distrusting of this army, small though it might be, as they had been of the one that had left just two days before.

Chapter 2

Some months after its delivery from the Norse militia, the township and the area surrounding it were back to normality. It was true that most working lives had gone on much as usual during the occupation because this had suited the Danes as much as the local people, but there had been little to do in the fields after the harvest had been gathered and under a strict curfew no personal contact, even between neighbours, had been allowed except on matters of business.

So now, for the first time in weeks, Athyll was able to relax his vigilance to some extent. As second in command to Sir Edwig he had been housed with the merchant weaver. At first this had pleased him until he began to receive the attentions of the two daughters, Lallage the elder and her sister Hella. They attended his every needs, cooking his favourite foods, washing his clothes. All this was at least bearable as he was out most of the day. Then, now that he had more time, he decided to take a bath. The two scampered round in great excitement, preparing the water and bringing clean cloths with which to dry himself.

It was not unusual for women to carry out this task but only for the menfolk of their family and not for strangers. Now that everything was ready they stood waiting in anticipation. He smiled politely and told them he was ready to take his bath. Hella the younger blushed and was pushed roughly out of the room. Lallage remained.

Since Athyll now saw that it was her intention to stay he stripped slowly. She stood her ground and watched him, unabashed, until he was naked. Now her cheeks reddened slightly and her breath came slightly faster. He took a large cloth from the edge of the bathtub. 'Thank you, Lallage — I have everything I need now,' he said softly. She wrongly took the tone of his voice to mean that he was as embarrassed as she and blushed more deeply.

'Very well, but please call if there is anything more that you require, Sir Athyll,' she said, giving him a title that he did not have without intending to flatter him. To her, all handsome men in mail and with a horse and sword must be knights. He nodded and after a further hesitation she left him to himself. As he clambered into the wooden tub he heard Lallage scolding her sister, who had obviously been listening at the door, and he laughed so much he finally fell into the water.

That night, Athyll was woken out of a deep and dreamless sleep by a gentle touch on his shoulder. A slim, white shape stood by his bed.

'Sir Athyll, it is Lallage,' she whispered. He sat up and saw that she was trembling and he had no doubt about the purpose of her visit. As he considered her, thinking how best to deal with the girl, she went down on her knees and put her hands together as in prayer. At last he got out of his bed and gently raised her to her feet.

'Listen to me, girl. This is very wrong and were I to tell your father he would deal with you very harshly,' he told her sternly. She looked up at him. As the tears came to her eyes he added: 'If you go quietly back to your room no more will be said. Now, please leave.'

The tears came in a rush now and he waited a moment for her to recover. Then, after she had wiped her eyes with the back of her hand and mumbled something which he took to be an expression of regret, though not necessarily an apology, he led her from the room. He waited at the open door to make sure of her departure, then returned to his bed.

He rose early so that he would breakfast alone. He had no wish to meet any members of the household and he was pleased that this proved to be the case. Having eaten, he decided to spend the day on his own and called for a servant to saddle his black stallion.

It was a bright, crisp Spring day with a promise of more warmth later on. He left the town and before long was enjoying the blossoming trees and the lush, green glades of the forest, the air fresh and pure and invigorating. It was so pleasant that he dismounted and, whilst his horse chewed on the rich verdure, he sat by a tree and drank ale from a leather bottle which had been carried on the saddle. He must have dozed because when he awoke the horse had gone.

CHAPTER TWO

He stood up and began to look for Surgel by tracing its hoofprints in the soft earth. After he had gone some distance he heard a whinny and followed the sound. It led him to a clearing and, standing by a tree, was a bay mare but no sign of his horse. He went to the mare and could see that she was holding one of her back legs off the ground and, as he lifted it, he could see that the animal was lame. He looked around him, then walked on to where he could see the sun glinting on the water. Suddenly the trees cleared and in the middle of a small lake a naked figure was splashing about.

He watched for some moments with amusement as he saw that it was a young woman. She had short, blonde hair, like a man, and small breasts. When she caught sight of him she attempted to cover herself; she called out something which he could not understand. He realised that this person must be the owner of the horse but how they came to be here in the middle of the forest, miles from any habitation, was something he wanted to know.

'I see your horse is lame — perhaps I can help,' he shouted back. She trod water and stared at him but ignored his call. She turned and looked toward the other side of the water and swam vigorously to it. Rising slowly out of the water with her back to Athyll now, she must have realised that she was no better off because her clothes and horse were still close by him. Finally she came back and ignoring him she swept past and went to her horse. She spoke to it gently — again he did not understand her — then took some clothing from bags on the saddle.

Athyll remembered Surgel. Leaving the girl to dress he went back into the forest. He stood there and whistled several times and at last there was the faint sound of hooves. Athyll whistled again and the big black horse thundered into the clearing and pulled up to nudge his master.

Back at the pool the girl had dressed but not, as he had expected, in the modest gown and veil of a woman but the leather coat, breeches, and boots of a man. And on her head was a soft leather helmet which covered her hair completely. She looked every inch a man, though youthful, and could have been anything from a bowman to an army messenger.

As a glimmer of the truth dawned on him he went to her with the intention of taking her captive and getting the whole story from her. As he seized her he felt a sharp kick on his shin and he had to tighten his grip as she tried to get out of his grasp. As she did so she slipped on the damp ground and pulled him down on top of her. As they struggled he strengthened his grip and she screamed as she tried to free herself. Finally he proved the stronger and she lay panting, mouthing something which he now realised was Norse,

15

then spat at him. When the outburst had subsided he rolled her over on to her stomach and, reaching for some handy twine, he managed to tie her wrists, at least until something better could be found. She lay there, still breathless, and he went to look at the mare.

He found a lump on the hock which was painful when pressed and would have to be attended to but, after walking the horse round a few times, he thought it might be able to travel the five or six miles back to Nottingham provided they went slowly. Another struggle ensued as he tried to get her up on Surgel's back but an exasperated threat to leave her in the forest, without her horse, seemed to quieten her and it also told him that she did understand some English. So, at last, they slowly made their way out of the forest toward the town, though from time to time she would angrily mutter something and once he caught the words 'Saxon pig'.

It was dark when they eventually reached Nottingham, for which Athyll was thankful since there was no-one to stand and stare at the strange sight of one horse carrying a man and a woman and another following. He went straight to Sir Edwig's quarters — a comparatively large place with stone foundations and stone walls, with roofing of wooden shingles in place of the usual thatch.

Sir Edwig was about to sit down to a meal and was surprised to see Athyll — even more so when he produced his captive who had been standing outside the range of the flickering fire light, the candles on the table being only of benefit to those using it. He stared at the girl and Athyll pushed her closer to the man. She opened her mouth, about to speak, then stopped herself. Sir Edwig finished his glass of wine in one gulp. He nodded to Athyll, inviting an explanation.

'I found her alone in the forest, sir. It seems her horse went lame and, as you can see, she is dressed like a soldier. I think she must have been with the Danes going north but had fallen back when her horse could not carry on.'

The thought of a woman dressed as a serving man angered Sir Edwig. He stood and his big frame towered over the girl even though she herself was quite tall.

'What is the meaning of this? Explain yourself, girl,' he shouted.

She glared at him, her blue eyes hard and unblinking. But still she said nothing.

'Answer me — what are you doing here in Mercia?' he asked again.

She looked away now — up at the ceiling, at Athyll, anywhere except at Sir Edwig. He raised his hand and brought it sharply across her face. As she stared at him in surprise — this was the first time she had been struck by any man — a red weal appeared on her cheek. Then the realization came to her and she kicked out at Sir Edwig. Athyll, standing close by, caught her foot just as it reached the Knight's leg, and she fell to the floor with a yell of pain as she hit the hard surface. She tried to struggle to her feet but, as her hands had been tied more strongly behind her, she found this difficult. Now, lying there, she uttered three Norse words which even some of the most vulgar Danish soldiery might have hesitated to use, indicating an act which both men could commit on themselves.

Sir Edwig returned to his table. 'We'll keep her here until we can discover more about her. Go on, take her away and lock her up.' Then, as the man pulled the girl to her feet, he shouted, 'And for God's sake get her some woman's clothes to wear.'

Athyll found a woman servant, who flew into a panic after being given instructions to look after this strange person whose like she had never seen before. However, a room was found and some rough clothes brought to her. The woman chattered on to the girl, telling her what to do, unable to understand that the girl did not speak her language. The girl flung the clothes onto the bed and demanded food. The poor servant woman stared uncomprehendingly. Athyll had returned now and the woman turned to him in some distress.

'I can't make out what she says, zur — I can't make 'er out at all.'

Athyll had just come from Sir Edwig and they agreed that the Danish girl's presence be kept within the bounds of the immediate household whilst they were trying to get some knowledge of her background. So the less the servants knew the better. He turned to the girl.

'What is it now?' he asked.

She hesitated for a moment, then put her hand to her mouth. 'Meat, drink.'

Athyll ordered the woman to fetch some water. 'You will get drink but no food until you tell us more about yourself,' he told the proud figure standing before him in arrogant defiance. But for all that she seemed to the man to be very feminine and vulnerable at this moment. He moved closer toward her and sat her gently on the rough bed. She jumped up and moved away from him. Athyll shrugged and went to the door.

'Very well then. No talk, no food,' he said, over his shoulder.

'Wait, come,' she called. He turned back into the room and waited.

'My name Medrin,' she said.

'Yes?' Athyll wanted to know more.

'My name Medrin,' she repeated.

'Why were you with the Danish army?' he asked.

She hesitated. 'I want fight Saxon.'

'Why?'

There was no hesitation now. 'Hate,' she said simply.

Berta, the servant, returned with the water and interrupted them. Athyll told her to bring some bread now and left them, reminding the servant that a close watch had to be kept on the girl at all times.

Although Athyll realized he had not had the whole story from his captive he was satisfied with what he had got and the rest would soon follow.

The Danish force, after it had left Nottingham, rapidly made its way to York where the intention was to join up with more of its men and then to use the time gained by its withdrawal from Nottingham to prepare for an invasion of East Anglia. They had gone some forty miles when two men who knew the truth about Medrin noticed that she was not with the main body. They dropped back to the rear of the column, thinking that she had had to leave to attend to her personal needs. But after some time they became concerned when she had not appeared.

'I fear that something must be wrong, Herotan,' said Sigbert, a squat, broad-chested man with hard, piercing eyes.

Herotan agreed, 'What can be done?'

Sigbert considered. 'We must find Medrin before she suffers any harm at the hands of the Saxon.'

'It may be too late, Sigbert,' suggested the more cautious Herotan.

His companion scratched his short, greying beard. 'You may be right but we must go back to look for her.' He reined his horse and turned back in the direction of the forest. 'Remember, we have responsibility for her safety,' he called and spurred his horse into a gallop, Herotan following without much enthusiasm. He had always thought the notion of a woman joining the noble Vikings was a foolish and dangerous one. Even though he was fully aware of the reasons, these had not removed his doubts.

Now that the small Anglo-Saxon force had become accepted and Nottingham had returned to normal, a group of travelling players arrived in the town to entertain the citizens who had been denied any sort of simple pleasure during the long winter months. When they arrived a space was cleared in the market square and they set up their places. They waited until a sufficient number of people had assembled, particularly children, then began their performance. First there were the women dancing to the pipes and lute and, when they stopped to rest, came the juggler; the first with wooden balls but the second with sharp, curved knives which he tossed into the air and caught by the handles as they fell, one being skilfully scooped up as it almost touched the ground. The puppet show pleased the children and some adults began to drift away until a man with a large brown bear appeared and they scurried back into the crowd.

The bear was on a long chain and the man was beating a small drum to which it danced and clapped its hands; the performances being repeated, wide-eyed children staying to see the same thing again and again.

Athyll had now decided that it was time to join the rest of his men with the King in Winchester and had obtained Sir Edwig's approval for the move. But there was the problem with the Danish girl-soldier, Medrin. What was to be done about her? Sir Edwig was indifferent, having other and more important matters to occupy his attention, so the onus for her had been placed firmly on Athyll's shoulders.

'Why don't you wed her and make her a good Christian?' Bowood had told him, laughingly.

The solution seemed to be that he would have to take her to Winchester with him and there he might be able to find some place for her. He was not quite sure what it would be but she had accepted women's clothes and had become more docile and obedient. And now that her horse had recovered after the blacksmith had skilfully removed the lump from its hock, and the travelling players were occupying the attention of most people, Athyll took the opportunity to saddle up and quietly leave with Medrin whilst it was still daylight. However, they were seen by the two sisters, Lallage and Hella, going home after watching the players. Lallage's lips set in a hard line — she had been spurned for a common servant girl and she would never forget the slight. From now on, she vowed, she would take everything from men and give nothing.

Three merchants — two elderly and the other a young man — the worse for drink and sitting on their horses unsteadily, were making their way to Nottingham from their trading places in Shrewsbury. They were now four miles east of the town and the elderly men had to stop, then decided to rest for a while.

Sigbert and Herotan, hearing voices, pulled up their horses and listened. The sound was possibly one or two hundred yards away. Sigbert indicated silence to the other man and dismounted. Quietly they moved forward, changing direction as they got nearer to the sound of the men talking — there was even a loud belch to help them place their position.

The two older men were sitting with their backs to a tree but the young man was still mounted. He was urging them to get back on their horses, being impatient to move and get to Nottingham. But the mixture of mead and wine was having more effect on them and they were quite content to stay where they were, at least for a while longer.

The two Danes struck quickly. Sigbert made for the men by the tree and within seconds they had been throttled by two large hands gripping their throats with a force which would have killed a stag. Herotan went for the horseman and caught his right arm to stop him from reaching for the dagger in his belt. But the horse reared and came down heavily on the Dane's foot. He swore loudly and had to release the arm, then a well-made leather riding boot hit him in the stomach. He doubled up in pain as Sigbert came up on the other side of the rider. He grabbed a leg but the man reared his horse again — it had to be released and the horse shot forward and galloped off, soon to be out of sight.

Later that day, only two hours after Athyll had left, the two men entered Nottingham dressed in the clothes of the dead merchants, convinced that this was the most likely place for Medrin to be and determined to find her. The players were still giving their performances and another group of dancers had been added to the attractions, so it was a fairly simple matter for them to wander through the crowds without drawing too much attention to themselves.

They were not to know that the young man who had eluded them had arrived before them. And it was their misfortune that he saw them and watched them make their way from house to house as if in search of something. He wasted no time in getting assistance and the two were taken immediately to Sir Edwig.

After a summary trial in which they were damned by the clothes they wore, their scant knowledge of English — they said nothing — and the evidence of the merchant, they were condemned to death. But instead of the

CHAPTER TWO

usual death by arrow they were taken the next morning to the nearest tree and hanged, whilst the soldier holding a battle-axe announced their crimes to a cheering, happy crowd.

Chapter 3

The first thirty miles or so of Athyll's journey to Winchester were uneventful and made in silence. It was late March, the day pleasant but with a mild north-east wind behind them, and after some hours travelling they stopped for a meal and a rest. Medrin was very attentive, preparing food, and when they had eaten and finished off the remains of mead from a stone bottle, she attended to the horses and drew water for them.

Athyll watched with amusement, not deceived at all by this uncharacteristic behaviour. He deliberately invented tasks for her in order to test just how far she was prepared to go to present this picture of willing assistance. She carried out all the work without a murmur, even with a smile, and he knew that she suspected his purpose. No fool she, he told himself, as well as being an excellent horsewoman and no mean fighter.

It was now only an hour before dark and Athyll decided to continue the journey until he found a suitable place to spend the night, preferably under cover. Had he been on his own it would have been a simple matter to stop at a farmhouse or cottage and ask for shelter; accompanied by a Dane, female though she might be, would be a different situation. There would have to be explanations and the attitude of Anglo-Saxon peasants toward Medrin would be unpredictable.

Eventually he came to a wood. It provided some cover and Athyll made a bower from the branches of trees, with a roof of ferns and moss. Once the girl had settled down he had to keep watch so he sat beside her. Though liable to doze from time to time he was a light sleeper and would awake on her making the least movement. And so it was that she slept the whole night through, awaking refreshed, whilst her guard had dozed fitfully, fortunately not an uncommon experience so he was none the worse for it.

Travelling all the next day and with another night stop, they were now almost within sight of their destination. At midday on the third day, after a final stop, they were standing by the bank of a stream and Athyll's attention was distracted by a hawk circling and suddenly swooping on some animal in the tall grass nearby. Medrin was nuzzling her horse and talking softly to it. She saw his interest in the bird, jumped on to the saddle-less horse and spurred it into a trot, then a gallop.

Athyll was not slow to react. Whistling to the stallion he ran with it and, catching the long mane, swung himself on to its back. Medrin saw him following and looked anxiously round. The stream was too wide to jump, the only course for her was to continue along the narrow bridle path and hope for something unexpected to happen, such as her captor falling off his horse and breaking his neck, or at least a leg.

Her wish was not to be. In the unequal chase Athyll's horse soon caught up with the mare only recently recovered from a damaged hind leg. The man passed her and pulled up so suddenly that Medrin only just saved herself from falling off by putting her arms round her horse's neck. Straightening up again, she spat a string of abuse at the man and tried to lash out with the reins but they were not long enough to reach him.

'You made a mistake — you should have taken the stallion,' he told her as he led her back to the spot where they had left their equipment.

As she was saddling her horse she turned to him and laughed. It was the first time he had seen this and her face took on a different look which was pleasant to see.

'You waste time,' she said at last. He waited to hear the reason why and she went on, her face set in the familiar grim expression again, 'Guthrum, the leader, will come.'

Since the return of King Ethelred with the news of the relief of Nottingham, Winchester had been an active city given over to festivities of every kind. On the day that Athyll and Medrin rode in, a procession was making its way to the Cathedral and an ox and several sheep were being roasted in the main square in readiness for the feast which would follow the service of celebration.

CHAPTER THREE

Medrin was attracted by the smell of cooking meat and edged her horse through the crowd, watching the young man tending the fire and the long spit with its crude handle at one end. She held out her hand and smiled at the good-looking youth. She wore a headdress of common brown cloth and a flowing gown of the same material — the clothes of a serving girl — but how did such a person come to be riding a magnificent thoroughbred horse? She pointed to her mouth and smiled again. He decided she must be a highborn lady in disguise who was joking with him. He pulled off a piece of meat, not yet properly cooked, and handed it to her; she held the meat in her hand, defying Athyll to take it from her. He shrugged and, taking the bridle of her horse, led her out of the crowd which had been watching with some interest.

As they entered the courtyard of a large house with local stone, a watch-tower at its peak and the bowman on guard instantly alert, she pulled her horse up sharply.

'Who is this place, Saxon?' she snapped. He ignored her and moved on to the entrance. Immediately a servant appeared and Athyll dismounted, in-dicating to Medrin that she should do so. She remained where she was. The puzzled servant went to take her horse but she pushed him away with her foot. Athyll moved quickly. He reached up and, grabbing the girl's waist in his strong hands, lifted her bodily off the horse. She yelled and struggled but the grip only tightened. At last she ceased to resist and he led her to the large, elaborately panelled wooden door which stood open.

Inside Athyll waited and it was not long before a tall, richly dressed woman appeared.

'Who are you and what are you doing here?' she demanded, eyebrows arched in displeasure.

'Forgive the intrusion but I am Athyll of York and I wish to see the Earl of Bedford,' he told her politely but resenting her manner.

'Lord Bedford is not here, he is attending the service in the Cathedral,' she replied briefly.

'Then to whom am I speaking?'

The woman paused for a moment, her eyes on Medrin. 'I am the Lady Bedford.' Another pause. 'Now, what is the purpose of your visit and who is this person?' pointing at the girl.

Athyll hesitated, looking down at her standing at his side. Again she had the look of helplessness, though it quickly passed under his gaze and her mouth set in a hard line. He wondered just how much she understood about what was happening.

'She is the main purpose of my visit, my lady,' he said at last.

'Then you must explain to me.' Lady Bedford turned and swept past them, clearly wanting them to follow. They did so and found themselves in a low-ceilinged room with a fireplace set in the wall and barely furnished with a table and chairs. Lady Bedford seated herself and Athyll gave an account of himself and his charge. At the end of it she contemplated them both with her chin resting on one hand — with the other she tapped the arm of the chair restlessly.

After some moments of thought, she said, 'I do not think you have acted wisely in this matter, young man, but it is clearly a case with which Lord Bedford will have to deal.'

Athyll had given her only the briefest facts and he thought that this needed an answer. 'I believe I had no choice, my lady. Sir Edwig of Bowood placed full responsibility on me for this woman. And I believe we can get some valuable information from her once she can be persuaded to talk. I also think that she is no common person but one of high birth and is therefore entitled to the consideration due to her.'

Lady Bedford stood, his equal in height. 'That will be determined by my Lord — in the meantime she will be taken to a room in the servant's quarters and be kept under lock and key. You, sir, will attend Earl Bedford at his pleasure.'

That was the end of the meeting and she left them. Medrin was taken away and, when she was left alone in a small, windowless room, she anxiously thought about what was going to happen to her. When she had to leave the Danish force going north, she had expected a search to be made for her once her absence had been noticed; now she realised that was not happening and she was on her own, at the mercy of those with whom her people were at war. She sat on her rough bed and tears of frustration and despair filled her eyes. She thought of Athyll, the Saxon enemy, and how, perversely, she had felt no fear of him. Now she knew instinctively that she was being taken out of his care. He had asked her to tell him about herself. She had not done so but now, perhaps, the time had come to do so.

The rest of the day being taken up with feasting and dancing, it was not until the following morning that Medrin and Athyll were brought before Edwig. The main hall of the manor had been cleared except for a long table

covered with an ornate silk cloth, on which his coat of arms were embla-
zoned. Lord Bedford sat in the centre; on his right were Sir Galwain of
Wantage and Ethelstan, a monk. Also seated were Sir Olfrith, and Egbert, a
wealthy citizen of Winchester. Standing close by was another monk,
Orfran, who was there to act as clerk and who had some knowledge of
Norse; his main occupation being to convert Danes who had been captured
or had decided to stay in the areas which had been conquered.

Medrin stood in the centre of the hall, a stark figure. Athyll was standing
some way from her but within speaking distance of the clerk. Bedford
looked around him and, satisfied that all was in order, he told Orfran to
explain to Medrin that the assembly was a court and called by him as the
King's officer. This the monk did and Medrin, trembling slightly, said that
she understood. After she had given her name and age, Bedford contemplated the girl. He had to admit to himself that he was puzzled. Murderers,
thieves, robbers, traitors he had had to deal with in plenty, but nothing like
this before.

Then: 'It has been reported by Athyll of York that he discovered you in
the forest of Nottingham and he believes you had been travelling north with
the Danish army. Is this true?' Bedford asked.

Orfran translated. Medrin replied unhesitatingly, 'Yes.'

'How was it that a young woman such as yourself was able to join an
army?'

Medrin hesitated. This was a more difficult question to answer since it
involved other people, such as her uncle Guthrum, leader of the Danish
army in Mercia, who had given his approval. She had been prepared to give
certain information about herself, but not if it concerned others of more
importance and the security of Danish forces. 'My father had no sons but I
was as good as any male child,' she said at last with some spirit. 'I wanted to
fight the Saxon and when I was old enough I was able to do so.' This was
true to a point and what it did not reveal was that her father was Gortvan,
brother of Guthrum — her mother had died at her birth — and that he had
been killed in a raid on the coast of Kent some four years previously. After
many entreaties of Guthrum, and a self-imposed winter in the open when
she was sixteen years old to prove her strength and courage, he had agreed
to her accompanying his army on this latest expedition. But there had been
conditions — she was to take a horse, carry no arms and be placed under the
protection of men whom he trusted. Her post would be that of courier

between Guthrum and his commanders. Medrin had agreed, with the mental reservation that she would decide what to do when she became involved in battle.

'Who was your commander?' Sir Galwain asked suddenly.

Another slight hesitation, then she said: 'I do not know his name.'

Athyll, listening carefully, recalled her words 'Guthrum, the leader, will come.' She had probably been referring to her commander but as he could see no point in the question he said nothing. He was also certain that no-one had much to fear from this young would-be warrior.

So the questions went on. Who were her parents? Where did she come from? To these she gave false answers — for the rest she claimed ignorance.

Eventually Medrin was led away by two servants and she cast a last despairing look at Athyll. A decision now had to be made about what action to take and Bedford invited opinions from the others. Ethelstan the monk was in favour of returning the girl to her own people but Bedford was not in support of this. Sir Olfrith, whilst not against the suggestion in principle, thought it impractical — the rest saw no merit in it at all. Egbert the merchant waited until all had had their say, then nervously cleared his throat.

'If I might be allowed a suggestion, my Lord, perhaps the girl could be placed in the care of my household. At this time my wife does have need of another servant to carry out menial duties and she would be kept under the closest watch.'

Bedford considered the man carefully. He had been handsome in his youth but now his cheeks were unhealthily florid and he was putting on too much weight, a fact which was emphasized by the large gown of blue cloth that he wore. Bedford did not like the man very much and suspected that he could not be trusted. But, however he looked at the proposal, he could find nothing against it and now that the others had given their views the final decision was his.

'Very well, then, let it be so. I charge you with the responsibility for the Dane and you will be answerable to me in all matters relating to her,' he told the merchant and with this concluded the session of the court.

Athyll left with a feeling of unease and disappointment. He had hoped that Medrin might have gone into Lady Bedford's service. Imperious and strict in manner she might be, but he had heard that she treated her servants fairly and they were not unhappy with her.

CHAPTER THREE

He decided he would see Medrin and try to reassure her that she might have had a worse fate than being put to work as a servant.

He found out from one of Bedford's staff where Egbert lived and he immediately made his way there. A buxom maid invited him into an ante-room with a smile when he told her that he had come from the Earl of Bedford and wished to see the merchant. She disappeared and it was not long before a plump woman in a gold-embroidered woollen dress and short veil came into the room. Her face was very red and she appeared to be under some stress.

'What is your business with my husband, sir?' Elsa asked breathlessly. Athyll explained and the woman sat suddenly on one of the chairs that were set against the wall. 'I'm afraid it is not possible for you to see this girl — it is out of the question,' she snapped.

'But why?' asked Athyll, striving to keep his irritation in check. 'I only wish to assure her that she will be looked after and given proper attention.'

'That is not a task for you, sir.'

'I intend to make it so.' He was about to add that he had brought the girl to Winchester and still felt some responsibility toward her when the woman interrupted him.

'Then you are wasting your time.' She stood, almost dwarfed by his height. 'I must ask you to leave at once, before my husband gets to know of your visit.'

There was nothing Athyll could do now, short of forcing his way and demanding to be taken to Medrin. In the small hallway on his way out he was met by Egbert, who had entered by the back door. His wife had also come into the hall, having followed Athyll. The three stopped and Egbert looked inquiringly at his wife. She explained rapidly who Athyll was, why he was there, and her forthright reply to his request. Egbert smiled and came over to Athyll, taking his arm and leading him to the door.

'I understand your concern, Athyll, and it is appreciated but quite un-necessary, I can tell you that without hesitation.'

Athyll was about to repeat his request to see Medrin but changed his mind. He was not one for pleading, preferring action to words. As he stepped out into the courtyard he glanced back at the house, wondering in which part she was being kept. There was no way of knowing; now, he told himself, there was one thing of which he was sure. Egbert the merchant had not seen or heard the last of him.

The next day other matters were occupying Athyll's mind. Sir Edwig had returned to Winchester with the remainder of the Wessex soldiers who had stayed with him in Nottingham. They included Black Edward, Harald and the rest of the bowmen; they had also brought with them — though it was more a case of not letting them leave without him — the tongueless man they had found in the wood. He had attached himself to this group of men and had made himself useful in many ways — even, sometimes, as a cook. They had dubbed him Gugg because of the sound he made when he tried to talk and, though he could neither read nor write, he was intelligent and learnt quickly.

These men were assigned to Sir Olfrith, with Athyll as his senior officer. He was ordered to report to Sir Olfrith and found Edwig was also there.

'This is Athyll of York, Olfrith,' Edwig told the broken-nosed, almost lame survivor of many battles. Olfrith considered the young soldier critically, correctly estimating his age at twenty-three years.

'Good,' he said at last. 'I've sent for you because we have news of the Danes. Messengers report that their main force has left York and is making for the Fen of East Anglia. Now, the King has also ordered that every man available must be prepared to protect Wessex and be ready for an attack. You have some men, more will be given, and it is your task to see that they are made ready to meet the Norse heathen.' He paused to take the jug of mead that Edwig handed to him. He drank deeply, taking his time, then looked up at Athyll. 'That is all — Go to your duty, man.'

Athyll bowed and made his departure after assuring Sir Olfrith that he was thankful to be of service to the King. He was also silently thankful that now his time would be fully occupied and the question of how Medrin was faring could be put to the back of his mind. As he swung himself up on to the patient Surgel's back, he had a sudden momentary vision of that last look that she had given him on being taken from the court and he spurred the horse into a gallop.

As he rode off to his camp the girl herself was lying on a rough bed covered with straw in a dark, windowless room. She was looking up at the ceiling, biting her lips so that they bled, to keep back the tears. Ever since Lord Bedford's decision to hand her over to the Egbert household she had been made to work but now she had unaccountably been taken back to her cell-like room. It was the time when the other servants ate — it did not occur to her to wonder why she was not getting any food because this was the last thing on her mind at this time. She sat up suddenly. She must find some way

CHAPTER THREE

of escape, there must be a way, she told herself. But even as she was thinking this the door opened and she was taken away to work again on the large tub containing the domestic washing.

Chapter 4

Months later the Danish Army, reinforced and led by Guthrum, moved south into East Anglia. His intention was to conquer the eastern seaboard of England, so ensuring protection for his men and supplies from the Norse countries, then to turn west into Wessex. It was not ambition which drove Guthrum on from one objective to another but a restlessness, a desire always to challenge Fate to give him victory or strike him down. His father had died when he was ten years old and the sight of the revered man laying on his funeral pyre was one which had haunted him ever since.

The march south continued with the occasional skirmish and the destruction of every monastery that the Danes came upon. But in Suffolk the resistance of the East Anglians was more fierce. Led by Edmund their king, they fought for two days, suffering many losses and Edmund himself was taken prisoner. He was brought before Guthrum and the other Danish leaders and their decision was that he should be put to death. Though his only offence was to oppose the invading Norsemen with all the power at his command, Edmund made no such plea and took the announcement of the sentence calmly.

The next day he was taken and bound to a tree. Six archers took aim and all the arrows pierced his body. Then a huge axe-man cut his bonds and, as he fell to the ground, the man brought his axe sharply down. Laughing loudly at the sight of the dismembered body, he was joined by those standing around. To these men there was no better sight than a dead Anglo-Saxon.

Guthrum now having assumed the crown of East Anglia, the invading forces turned their attention to the rich spoils of the Fen country. Peterborough and Ely abbeys went up in flames and their monks fled or were put to death amongst the ruins. From here the advance south continued and the Danes were ready to make their first attack on Wessex. They turned west and pushed up the Thames to Reading where its junction with the Kennet offered a base which required little fortification.

Whilst his army was being resupplied and resting at Reading, Guthrum was able to give some thought to Medrin. Before he left York he had received news of the execution of Sigbert and Herotan but he had heard nothing of her. He had a strong feeling that she had been taken south to Winchester and now, apart from the more important military purpose, he had hopes that with his continued advance he would take the city and find her there.

News of their rapid progress, the taking of Reading and existence of a force of Danes close to his capital had reached King Ethelred in time for him to muster Berkshire levies under the command of the ealdorman. Within three days of Guthrum's arrival this small force was sent out but in their first encounter with a Danish raiding party they were routed. Four days later a larger force, led by the King and his younger brother Alfred, confidently attempted a direct assault on the Danish positions but had to retire defeated because of the strength of the Norse defences.

The Danes, exploiting their advantage, moved out of Reading and in a battle at Ashdown on the Downs they were on open ground and were driven back to take refuge once again in Reading. Within two weeks Ethelred was defeated outside the town and had to retreat. So the battles continued, first this way and then that, though both sides used the Winter more in preparation for the coming Spring than in actual fighting. The Anglo-Saxon losses had been great and after the debilitating battles of the past months the men were exhausted. Then came the greatest blow of all, the death of their king, Ethelred. Now that Alfred had assumed the crown, his hope was that he would be able to gain a respite from the war for his people — there were so many things he could do for them in a time of peace.

So a meeting with Guthrum was arranged in an open field near Reading.

As they faced each other Alfred said: 'Thank you for attending — I am Alfred, King of Wessex, since the death of my brother, Ethelred.'

34

CHAPTER FOUR

Guthrum moved forward and held out his hand. 'And I am Guthrum, King of East Anglia, and commander of the Danish forces.'

Alfred, whilst having mental reservations about the claim to kingship of English land, grasped the outstretched hand in both of his and shook it firmly.

The meeting was carried out in an atmosphere of mutual respect, both kings being good judges of their fellow men. Alfred found Guthrum straight-thinking and blunt whilst the Dane found his opponent equally open and a good listener. So, finally, a cessation of the fighting was agreed, though neither was under any illusion that the war was at an end.

As he made to leave Guthrum remembered Medrin. 'There is one other thing, Alfred.' He paused, wondering how the other was going to take his request. Alfred nodded, waiting.

'I have a niece, Medrin, to whom I gave permission to join our forces in England. A little unwise of me, perhaps, but no matter — I have reason to suspect that she has been captured and is being held by your people. I would like you, Alfred, to find out if this is true, and if so to return her to me by whatever means you may find.' Alfred agreed to do this and whilst Guthrum went on his way to London he returned to Winchester, leaving at Reading a small garrison of his soldiers, reinforced by local levies, as had been agreed with the Danish King.

Having served for nearly a year in actions against the Danes, Athyll found himself one of the men left at the Reading base after the new king had returned to his capital. During this time Medrin had never been far from his thoughts, though he would not have admitted, even to himself, that his interest in her was any more than it would have been for another person needing help in hazardous times. The trouble was that he knew little or nothing about her after so long an absence. Nevertheless, he could not deny the uneasy feeling he had that all was not as it should be with her.

After thinking about it for what was for him a long time, Athyll made up his mind about what he should do. He saddled Surgel and rode out to the modest homestead that Sir Olfrith had made his temporary headquarters. He had not chosen his moment well — his commander was having a violent quarrel with the local provisioner over food supplies which had not been delivered or had mysteriously disappeared after delivery. The merchant insisted that he had delivered meat and other supplies and had enraged Sir Olfrith by suggesting that his men had taken the food. Whilst he knew that this did happen, he was not going to be reminded of it by a petty tradesman.

When Athyll arrived he was ordered to wait but could hear the row going on.

'I don't care what he says, sir, I wants money for what was left here by our handyman but only yesterday, sir,' the man was shouting.

There was a moment's silence, then the sound of a chair scraping the floor. 'And I tell you that I am not giving any of the King's good coin for foodstuffs which have not been seen by any — I say again — any of my men.' Another pause. 'Now go, before I call my guards and have you thrown into Reading's filthy jail.'

'But, sir, please, I swear . . .' The man's voice had now lost its truculence and was pleading. Olfrith cut him short by going to the door and shouting for the guard. As it happened the solitary man on duty had left to attend to a call of nature just before Athyll arrived. His presence proved unnecessary — the merchant rushed out of the room not waiting for any further reminder of his fate if he stayed.

Athyll waited a few minutes, then entered to find Sir Olfrith pouring a drink and quietly laughing to himself. On seeing Athyll standing before him his face resumed its normal expression. Athyll was encouraged by the fact that, as a professional soldier, his contempt for those in more conventional and peaceful work was well known.

He took his drink, then looked up at the younger man. 'Well, Athyll, I do not remember having sent for you.'

'No, sir, I wanted to speak to you.' Olfrith's greying eyebrows raised questioningly but he waited for the other to continue. 'I wish to request leave of absence for a month, sir.'

Olfrith sat back and roared with laughter. 'My God, you have a nerve, I'm damned if you have not,' he said at last, then went on: 'And what, pray, do you intend to do with the time — assuming that I give it to you?'

One thing that would be certain to stop leave from being granted was the truth. Athyll had already thought of that. 'My horse needs attention and I need rest to prepare for our next battle.'

It had been Olfrith himself who had warned his men that the present peace was only a temporary lull in the war. He nodded. 'Perhaps some leave could be taken but I think a month excessive.'

'The care of my horse might take most of that time, sir.'

CHAPTER FOUR

Olfrith sat back and considered the tall, slight figure before him. He had received news the previous day that Sir Edwig was on his way with reinforcements for his garrison and could afford to release Athyll, but he liked to test a man's mettle against himself.

Having gained his point Athyll left his camp the next morning. As he moved off a group of men came up to him. He reined in Surgel impatiently.

'Is it true more men be coming to Reading, sir?' asked Harald. From a gangling youth he had become a man after his first experience of battle. In the past months he had put on weight and had a full beard.

'Yes, I think that is so,' Athyll told him.

'Are you going to meet them sir?' asked Black Edward slyly, having heard that Athyll had leave.

Athyll looked down at him but did not bother to reply, aware that the big man already had the answer. He turned the horse's head and moved off, slowly at first, then broke into a gallop.

'I hope he stays in 'chester,' muttered the big bowman. He did not like Athyll for reasons which he could not have explained but were to do with the fact that he was not a Wessex man and rode a fine horse instead of walking. Harald turned on him fiercely.

'That man is a good soldier and loyal to the King. I seen him risk his life not once but many times up against them Danes,' he shouted.

'So we all did,' Black Edward yelled back and was about to make a lunge at Harald but thought better of it. He was tired and, in spite of his bulk, he knew the younger man had the advantage of him. As he walked away he was content to mouth his favourite vulgar expressions and leave it at that.

Though her first weeks at the merchant's house were as much as Medrin could bear they gradually improved. To her surprise she was moved to a room above ground and, though the window was small, there was some light. Then, instead of rough clothing of sacking she was given a gown of wool much softer on her skin, which had developed a rash. In addition, her duties became lighter and more pleasant to carry out. Having more contact with other people in the house was also better for her and enabled her to improve her English, particularly with the help of Ellen, a servant who did much the same work as herself. In spite of all the talk about her being a despised Dane, the girl felt sorry for Medrin and was the only one of the household who would give her any assistance. Nonetheless, even that had to be done quietly and discreetly.

An older and more experienced person might have suspected the motive behind the improvement. Medrin accepted it, believing it to be only right and natural; that her first experience had been a mistake and recognised as such. But though she went about her work much happier, she still had dreams of escape, mixed with frequent visions of a tall young Anglo-Saxon captain, reddish-brown hair blowing in the wind, smiling at her. These had been less frequent after her release from her underground hovel but still persisted.

As the days passed and she grew stronger and more womanly, her only regret was that she could not leave the house. More freedom did not include this and from time to time a check would be made on her; she never knew when that would happen. The only fresh air she got was from open windows and this irked her as a person who had spent so much of her life in the open. From an early age the trees and lakes of Scandinavia had been the only company she had had. As she grew older and began to attract the attention of young males she still preferred to be by herself, in her natural element.

On a night when another servant was ill Medrin had to serve a meal to Egbert, who always ate alone. He seemed to watch her every movement as she went about the work and it made her feel uncomfortable but she gave the man no indication that she was aware of it. Reaching over the table to pour his wine he put his arm around her waist, then raised his hand to her breast. She reddened and pulled quickly away. The meal was finished now but it was his rule that the server waited until dismissed. Medrin stood by a small table as the minutes dragged, dreading the moment when he would rise from the table.

He had taken his fourth glass of wine before he eventually got up and made his way out of the room without a word or look in her direction. Medrin thankfully cleared the remains of the meal and went to her room. She undressed and was combing her hair, now grown long, when the door opened. Egbert stood there, a little unsteadily. Medrin caught up her dress and covered herself but he lurched toward her and pulled it away.

Medrin's recollection of what followed was of a violent movement; a mouth that was sometimes close to hers then on other parts of her body; of searing pain. As she struggled he rolled to her side and she was able to free herself and jump from the bed. Blood was issuing from her and when she saw it a violent rage shook her. She moved toward him and saw his finely woven tunic on the floor — beside it was his belt with its ornate clasp and dagger. She snatched the dagger from its sheath and plunged it once, twice, into the body on the bed. She threw it down, suddenly realising what she had done, then she was in headlong flight in the dark, airless passages. Once she got lost and had to retrace her steps but she eventually found the room which Ellen shared with three other servants.

Woken up out of a deep sleep, it was not until she saw the bloodstained undergarment that Ellen became aware of Medrin.

'Please, Ellen, please help me,' she gasped.

The girl, frightened by something she did not understand but knew was wrong, sat up. 'What is it — what's happened?' she whispered.

'Not here — not here,' Medrin told her, clasping her arm.

Looking down at her the Wessex girl saw the tearstained face raised imploringly. She jumped out of bed, dressed quickly and hurried Medrin out of the room. Leaving by a little-used back stairway they got out onto the road. It was rough on their unshod feet but it was a warm Autumn night and dry. Medrin staggered and fell once but after some time they stopped at a small cottage. No more than a hovel, it had two rooms. Sleeping in one were a middle-aged man and a woman and the man was none too pleased at being woken up.

Ignoring her father's complaints, Ellen took Medrin through to the other room. Cluttered though it was she found a place on the floor for the Danish girl and cradled her head in her lap. It took some time to make her parents understand that Medrin had fallen down the stairs and injured herself but they let her attend to the girl as best she could after she had promised that Medrin would not stay too long. Blessing the fact that they were a couple of simple people who did not question what they had been told, Ellen returned to the manor.

She had not been missed — the question now was what would happen when the Dane's absence was discovered. Though Medrin had been unable to tell her what had happened, Ellen surmised the truth and as she got into her rough bed she wondered what the morning would bring.

Chapter 5

When King Alfred had arranged a truce with Guthrum at Reading he realized that the Danes had withdrawn with a view to gaining time and a firmer footing for further attacks. But his concern was for his people and now that he was King he pledged himself, as a Christian, to devote himself to the welfare of those over whom he had been placed to rule. To him this meant living a life of self-sacrifice and seeing that justice was done. It did not mean that he was not prepared to fight in defence of all those things he held dear, but he was prepared to set aside all dreams of conquest in order to achieve good government and the education of his people. This vision of the future also showed him that peace was necessary in order for it to be achieved.

The King's first task was to organise the defence of his realm of Wessex, which stretched from London and its surrounding country to beyond Exeter, by guarding against any inroads from Mercia and East Anglia to the north. He also provided for a better organisation of military service by improving the lot of his regular soldiers and giving them better equipment; preparing against invasion from the sea, he formed a closer union with the bordering kingdoms of Kent and Sussex and was building a new fleet.

These measures taken by the new King created an atmosphere of hope and joy when the people of Wessex became aware of all the activity which was putting new life into their country. A totally different spirit was replacing one of war-weariness and despair of the future, and it was this spirit that Athyll met when he rode into Winchester.

As Surgel made his way slowly through crowded streets, women waved to him, men doffed their hats and there were smiling faces everywhere.

Realizing that he must have been presenting an untidy sight, with his matted hair, several days growth of beard and travel-stained clothing, with his horse in equally bad shape, Athyll thought this greeting was being given to him simply as a victorious soldier. But later, after he had left the stallion with a farrier and had found himself a lodging with other cavalrymen in the city, he noticed that the air of optimism and pleasure was everywhere.

Enjoying the new spirit and having eaten a good meal, Athyll's thoughts turned to Medrin. The mental image of her straight, slim body, clear blue eyes set in a face of faultless complexion, increased his happiness at the thought of seeing her again. But now it was early afternoon, a time when he would be unlikely to see her, so he had to curb his impatience and wait.

It was three hours later when he found himself at the door of the merchant's house and hardly able to contain his excitement. It was opened by a servant who looked up at him fearfully and, as he stepped into the hallway, the atmosphere suddenly become chill and menacing. He had announced himself to the girl and his wish to see the merchant, now she hurried off without having spoken a word. Athyll looked around him, tapping his leg impatiently, when a sudden fear gripped him. He could not explain it to himself, it was totally unlike any other fear he had known before.

He did not have to wait long. A male servant appeared and took him straight to Egbert. The man was sitting in a high-backed chair with his left arm heavily bandaged. He indicated a seat but Athyll declined it.

'Now, young man, may I know the purpose of your visit?'

Athyll was in no mood for time-wasting talk. 'Some months ago I brought a young Danish girl to Winchester and she was put in your care by the Earl of Bedford. I believe I have a right to know how she is faring and it is my intention to stay until I have seen her and I am satisfied that she is being well treated.'

Egbert's eyebrows raised slightly. 'Your request exceeds the bounds of politeness, sir, but even if I was prepared to grant it that would not be possible.'

'And why not?' Athyll's face flushed with suppressed anger.

There was a pause whilst the merchant studied the soldier. 'It seems to me that your interest in this girl, a Dane and a prisoner, far from being admissible is a distinctly unhealthy one.'

'You have not answered my question. Why is it not possible for me to see the girl?' Athyll asked, still striving to keep his temper.

CHAPTER FIVE

There was another pause while the man took a drink from a glass of wine. Then he looked up at Athyll, his face distorted with ill-feeling. 'Because she is not here — because she escaped and now must be on her way back to her own Godless people.'

Athyll stared in disbelief. Then it slowly came to him that the man must be telling the truth.

'So you see, you have been wasting your time,' the merchant told him and took another drink. Athyll noted with distaste the look on the man's face, then made to leave. Remembering something, he turned back to Egbert.

'You seemed to have injured your arm. Might I ask how that happened?'

A pair of red-rimmed, unhealthy eyes considered Athyll thoughtfully for a moment. 'Once again I have to tell you that it is none of your business,' the merchant said at last, and went on: 'but I will tell you if only to get you out of my house. I was attacked and robbed in the street one night.' He stood a little unsteadily. 'Now, go before I have to put you out.'

But Athyll had heard enough and was already out into the hall. His one thought now was to find Medrin before she came to harm from any number of dangers she could meet trying to reach the Danish forces.

He started to walk away from the house when he was suddenly faced by Ellen. Having heard that he was with Egbert she had watched for him to leave and had slipped out into the street from a side door.

'Sir, I must talk with you,' she whispered and led the way through the crowded streets and a market until they were on a path well out of sight of the merchant's house.

'Well, girl, what is it?' Athyll asked impatiently. He had to wait until she caught her breath. Then: 'You are the soldier who caught the Danish girl?'

He nodded. He now recognised Ellen as the girl with the pleasant smile who had admitted him when he had first called at the house some months ago.

'Sir, one night last week she came to me and asked for my help. She was badly hurt.'

'Hurt? In what way?' put in Athyll quickly.

The girl looked up at him, tears in her eyes. 'She had a bad wrong done to her and was bleeding . . .' She paused to wipe her eyes with her rough sleeve, 'and I took her to my father's cottage. She only stayed a night and a day, sir, then she was gone.'

The statement, simple though it was, told Athyll all he wanted to know. The girl suddenly swayed and he caught her by the shoulders.

'Thank you, girl. Have you told any other person about this?' She shook her head. 'Good. Now go back to the house and remember not to say a word to another soul. Do you understand?'

'Yes, sir, but what are you going to do?'

'I'm going to find Medrin.'

Athyll's problem now was to find a horse as Surgel was still not fit to ride. He called at the farrier's forge but the man only had a mare that could be used. Athyll looked at it doubtfully. Though it might have taken him it would not have been able to carry two people. He declined to use it in spite of the man's insistence that it was a fine horse. He now had to search the city and at last found a fellow cavalryman, recently injured in a brawl with two other men, who was willing to lend Athyll his ten-year-old roan.

While it was still daylight he rode out of the city, fearful about Medrin and what might be happening to her, his mood now in stark contrast to the festival air of the place he was leaving, and determined to bring the merchant Egbert to justice. But, first, he had to find the girl and bring her back to Winchester.

Chapter 6

Athyll made good progress that day, covering some forty miles before he stopped at a lonely homestead, chosen for its isolation. A rather suspicious herdsman agreed to give him shelter for the night and food for himself and his horse. The man did not ask any questions so Athyll did not have to give an explanation for his solitary journey, yet there was an underlying atmosphere of hostility towards him which was unpleasant. Guarded attempts to get information about what was happening locally got only curt replies, or none at all. It became clear to Athyll that he would get little from the man, even if he had known something to tell.

The next morning he was pleased to move on, continuing to follow the route he thought Medrin would have taken to reach her own people. He was now travelling at a much slower speed, walking the horse most of the time and only rarely breaking into a trot. That night he spent in the open, having met only a solitary shepherd during the whole day, but later on the following day he came across a group of people — three men and a woman — whose wooden cart had become trapped when one wheel had rolled into a large hole in the ground. They were having difficulty and Athyll dismounted, offering to help. So, by tying a rope from the cart to the horse's saddle, they all got behind the wheel and pushed until it was pulled free with its load of a large barrel of ale. Athyll declined to have a drink when the barrel was quickly opened but seized the moment of goodwill to ask about any strangers they might have seen recently. There was a pause whilst the four thought about it.

'Yes, they was a youn' wumman us see this mornin',' said the eldest of the men, bearded and with bad teeth.

'What about her?' asked Athyll, concealing his excitement.

'She run away, diddun her. Must have been old Tog's face,' said the woman, nodding at the old man and laughing.

Athyll smiled too. 'And which way did she go?' The woman pointed vaguely to the south, not to the east where Medrin had been heading almost certainly until now. He checked with the woman again and she told him she was sure that was the direction.

The group now prepared to move ahead but Athyll turned his horse off the track into the thick shrub. Before him was the Weald of Sussex with no town or habitation of any sort that he knew or had even heard of. For some reason not hard for him to imagine, knowing of her recent experience, the Dane had lost her way and could be in even greater danger now that she had wandered off the beaten track.

The man searched the area for days without result. Then, after combing a thick wood for any sign of the girl, he came out into the open country again and could see a large building in the distance, surrounded by outhouses and with cattle and sheep grazing in the fields nearby.

He spurred his horse and soon reached the building. Dismounting, he walked about but there no was sign of anyone. Crossing the yard spattered with cow dung he banged loudly on a big door but there was no reply. Turning to go back to the horse, Athyll was now faced by two men, one of whom was holding the horse's bridle; the second had a pike in his hand. They were big men, very much alike except that one was heavily bearded and the other was not, and both were dressed in the simple woollen gown and breeches of the countryman.

Athyll, pleased to see someone, even though the attitude of the men was far from friendly, moved forward to meet them. He was met by the point of the pike being placed in his stomach by the bearded man.

'Who are you — what do you want with us?' The pike was pushed a little further as the man spoke.

'My name is Athyll of York and I . . .'

'York? Where is that place?'

'It is in Northumbria, I am a soldier serving the King of Wessex.'

'Oh! And who is the King?' put in the man holding the horse's bridle.

CHAPTER SIX

Athyll hesitated, puzzled by the question. Surely these people knew their own King. 'It is Alfred who has been King for nearly a year or more — you know that as well as I do,' he snapped.

'If you are a soldier what are you doing here?' asked the bearded man, still suspicious. Athyll explained as briefly as possible his search for Medrin, omitting the fact of her ordeal at the hands of Egbert, putting it simply that she had been ill and was to be returned to Winchester for her own protection. As for his own part, he told them how he had originally captured the girl and now felt a personal responsibility for her.

Whilst he had been talking two more men had come out of an outhouse and had stood listening. When he had finished one of the men, much older than the others and better dressed, ordered him to be taken into the building. It was a large barn with hay stacked untidily in one corner and a crude ladder leading to a loft. Athyll was taken up to the loft and his hands tied behind him. There he was left.

It was hours later and quite dark when the elderly man and another returned with a rough meal and something to drink. He introduced himself as Ulfric and said the other men were his sons — he also had a daughter-in-law who kept house for them. His manner was cold but polite.

'You will stay until morning and my son will also be here to make sure you do not leave,' he told Athyll and turned to go.

'But why? Why am I not allowed to go on my way?' he shouted after the man.

He went back to Athyll and put the flax torch he carried close to his face. 'I'm not happy with your story, and I intend to find out more before you go.' This was not the whole truth but it was the only satisfaction that the soldier was going to get for the moment. After the man had gone it was dark again and Athyll called out. There was not a sound from his guard and he thought he had been tricked — edging his way to where he believed the ladder to be, he wanted to try and break the bonds on his wrists. His feet soon fell over the edge of the loft floor, then he moved them along until he felt them touch the ladder.

He turned on his back and placed the thongs on the part raised above the floor and started to rub the bonds on it. Then he felt a sickening blow in his side and could just make out the dim shape standing above him. The man leaned over and pulled Athyll back from the ladder into a heap of straw; with a final oath and another warning kick he disappeared out of sight again.

All next day Athyll was left very much to himself and only saw another person when food and drink were brought to him. When darkness came it followed the pattern of the night before but with a different guard keeping a mysterious, unseen watch on him. But on the second day of his unexplained captivity Athyll demanded to be allowed to have a wash and this was granted. As the place he was taken to was near the main building and living quarters, he now demanded to see the elderly man. The request was made arrogantly of the two men with him and he waited for a hostile reaction. To his surprise it did not come and later he found himself face to face with Ulfric, the head of this strange household. He looked tired and was older than Athyll had thought but he sat upright in his chair. His eyes were alert, his gaze fixed firmly on Athyll.

In spite of that penetrating look he was not intimidated. 'I have been kept here against my will for some time and without any reason being given.' He paused and looked around him — all four men were now in the room. 'Now, tell me why,' he demanded.

Ulfric exchanged a glance with his sons. One of them, a thin, frail man who peered shortsightedly at everything, nodded to his father.

'You spoke of a Danish girl who ran away from Winchester — a girl called Medrin.'

'Yes — because she was ill and did not know what she was doing.' He was still trying to protect the girl's honour by not mentioning the assault on her.

'And you took it upon yourself to look for her?'

'Yes. I was on leave and free to do so — I did not think it would take long.'

Ulfric considered the young man coolly. 'Athyll of York, as you call yourself, we believe that you are not telling us the truth. We think that you attacked the girl — that is why she ran away from you — that you are now looking for her because you are afraid she will tell the truth about you . . .'

Athyll, stunned for the moment, suddenly interrupted the man with a shouted: 'Lies — these are damned lies!'

Ulfric stood up. 'We shall see.' He called a name several times and a woman appeared, dressed in a silk gown and a headdress of the same material.

'Is the girl ready?' he asked her.

The woman nodded. 'Yes, she is waiting now.'

'Then bring her to me.'

48

CHAPTER SIX

As the woman left the room Athyll stared in disbelief. Then it came to him that the girl was Medrin and that she had been here all the time. But what was all that nonsense about him having attacked her? He waited, calmer now.

After what seemed to be a long time to Athyll she came into the room followed by Ulfric's wife. She wore a clean grey gown, her hair had grown long and was pulled back and tied behind her. Her face was pale and drawn, she looked tired and there were dark rings under her eyes. She was so different from the girl he had last seen a year ago that the change shocked him. Ulfric motioned her to take his seat and she did so without looking up.

The old man pointed to Athyll. 'Do you know this man?' he asked Medrin.

She looked at him with lack-lustre eyes, then turned away again. 'Yes.'

'His name?'

She stared at the man as if she did not understand why he had asked the question, then she turned back to Athyll. 'He is Athyll — a soldier.' Suddenly she noticed that his hands were bound behind him. 'Why is he like this?' she asked, holding her wrists together.

Ulfric exchanged glances with his two sons. The bearded one shrugged his indifference and the other looked as though he did not understand Medrin's question. Ulfric turned back to her.

'Is this not the man who attacked you?'

Medrin looked from one to the other of the men standing before her, finally at Athyll, and her eyes filled with tears as understanding came to her. She jumped up and faced Ulfric, her tall frame trembling. 'No, it is not — he is not the man,' she told him quietly but firmly. Then, with more emphasis: 'Sir, he has done no wrong — you must let him go.'

Ulfric took her by the shoulders. 'Yes, Medrin, yes — that will be done but we had to know the truth about the man from you,' he said and led her back to his wife.

As the two women made to leave Medrin looked back at Athyll and he wanted to call out to her but no sound came and he stood helplessly watching her go.

The man was as good as his word and Athyll was released. No apologies were made for his treatment but an explanation was given that the Danish girl had been ill and they had had to wait before she could be brought to identify him and confirm his story.

He was given a room in the house and welcomed it, even the rough bed, as a big improvement on his condition of the last unpleasant hours. For the first time he had a meal that could properly be given a name — he ate roast sheep and drank mead and ale with relish, to the point of excess.

There had been little talking during the meal and, after the old man had excused himself and retired, the others continued with their drinking and were soon in a state in which nothing said made much sense. Athyll himself was beginning to feel the effects of the strong local wine so he left and made his way to his room a little unsteadily. The thought came to him, vaguely, that he would like to talk to Medrin, then he remembered that she was still needing rest. Reaching his room he threw himself on his bed. As he closed his eyes the vision of her came to him as he had first seen her, rising out of the water, naked as the day she was born, and with a haunting beauty.

Athyll spent the next few days having to kill time and fretting at the delay in moving on. His leave was now over but he was not so much concerned with that as the fact that Medrin was still unable to travel. So he went hunting for boar, practising archery and swordsmanship. He found he was left to carry out these activities alone as the men of Ulfric's household were busy with their own tasks. He found he had little in common with any of them anyway, so his isolation did not prove burdensome.

One day it rained heavily and he had to wander aimlessly round the place, but having to resist strongly the temptation to go to the women's quarters and see Medrin. However, the next day was fine and, after a light breakfast of bread and fresh eggs, he went for a walk in the wood. It was a bright, crisp day and he returned feeling invigorated and even more anxious to be on his way back to Winchester. He was met in the yard by the bearded son and was told that Ulfric wanted to see him.

Athyll ran into the house and found Medrin with the man. Her features still looked drawn but there was a bit more colour in her cheeks and she smiled when Athyll came into the room. He went to her and took her hands in his. Ulfric was also smiling.

'She has asked to see you,' he said briefly, then left them.

Athyll led the girl to a chair and knelt beside her. 'Medrin, what is it? You are looking better — are you able to leave with me now?'

She looked at him, the dark rings caused by sleeplessness and pain contrasting with the blueness of her eyes. 'Yes, Athyll, I am better but if you want me to go to Winchester I cannot.'

The man stood up. 'In God's name, why not?' he asked in surprise.

50

CHAPTER SIX

Medrin hesitated. The memory of that night still haunted her. 'You know well the reason,' she said, tears welling.

'Medrin, I can see no cause at all.' He paused. 'Unless it is because you are a Dane and escaped from the merchant's care. That was no crime, I can promise you.'

The tears came freely now. 'How can you say that — I killed the man. Don't you understand — I killed him,' she cried.

Athyll looked down at her pityingly. Once again he saw that unguarded look of defencelessness. He knelt and put his hands on her. 'Medrin, dear girl — Egbert is not dead, he lives,' he told her smiling. She looked up at him doubtfully.

'But — but I stabbed him, two, three times, I don't know how many.'

Athyll rose and lifted Medrin to her feet. 'Yes, but only to wound him. Believe me, I saw him and spoke to him long after you had gone from Winchester.'

Medrin placed her forehead on his shoulder but said nothing. When she looked up again she was smiling through the tears and the colour was coming back to her cheeks.

That evening a group of strolling players, passing by on their way to London, told of rumours that the Danes had invaded Mercia in force and that their fleet had been sighted off the south coast. Athyll's plan now was to make his way back to Winchester by a more direct route and, once Medrin had been settled safely, to join the King's forces now fighting in the heart of Mercia against an enemy that was posing a greater threat then ever to the people of the south.

Chapter 7

The varying accounts of the Danish advances into Mercia going around in the south were proving to be basically true, though they might have differed in their treatment of detail. Many people on the border of Wessex with Mercia believed the worst and left the area, some taking all their worldly possessions with them; others considered these were not worth the trouble of saving. Some went their way to the west, some south, but many put their hope in reaching the capital where they had heard there was sanctuary and food. Even more importantly, their King was there and they felt that they would be safe under the protection of his royal person and the army.

Guthrum the Dane, King of East Anglia, intended to destroy all the English kingdoms one by one. He had already achieved the conquest of East Anglia; he had made a brief incursion into Northumbria to assess the strength of its defences before an all-out onslaught; now he had invaded Mercia to achieve a firm base for the attack on Wessex which he believed would be his most difficult objective.

Moving rapidly from Ely and Torksey and meeting little resistance, Guthrum soon reached Repton in the heart of Mercia. His soldiers went through the town pillaging, looting and putting down women and children, as well as men, with spear and sword until the cobbled streets ran with blood. These were not Guthrum's orders but he had found it impossible to stop his men from committing these acts of barbarism, particularly when they were often urged on by his local commanders.

Once firmly installed in the town, he ordered that Burgred the King be brought to him. The meeting was short. Guthrum told the Mercian that he was no longer King and that he was to be banished and replaced by a Thane

THE VIKING GIRL

appointed by himself. This man, Thurdon, proved to be an ex-cavalryman of the Mercian army who had been wounded in an earlier battle with the Danes but preferred their more vigorous rule to that of the weak Burgred. At Guthrum's invitation he was now prepared to put himself in the Dane's service; the people were not told of their change of leader and Burgred's departure went unnoticed. And, in truth, they were too numb to care even if it had been so.

The day was mild as Athyll and Medrin went on their way — it was the kind of weather that reminded Medrin of her homeland, with the light of the sun reflecting on the pale leaves of late summer, foreshadowing the coming Autumn. Because of their slow progress they had gone but a few miles when they came face to face with a body of people; men and women, some carrying their small possessions, and young children in carts pulled by older children.

There were some hundred or more of these people and the soldier reined his horse in front of the leaders of the long column. His instinct was already warning him of danger.

'Father, what is it? Where are all these people going?' Athyll called out to a monk who was leading them. The man came forward and looked closely at Athyll and the girl sitting on the horse behind him.

'Who are you, sir, and why do you ask?' he wanted to know, holding his cross before him as he spoke.

'I am Athyll, an officer of cavalry serving King Alfred.'

The man noticed the helmet and the sword at his side, then looked again at Medrin. 'And this woman?'

Athyll paused, thinking of a credible answer.

'I am his sister,' put in Medrin quickly. 'I have been ill and he is taking me home to Winchester.'

The reply seemed to satisfy the monk and Athyll was grateful for the girl's quick thinking.

'So, what is happening?' he asked again.

'Well, there is a body of men moving east who are causing havoc by killing and ravaging as they go from place to place. These people you see had warning and left their homes to find safety,' the monk told him.

Athyll was puzzled. 'Who are these men — are they Danes?' This seemed unlikely to him but he had been out of touch with the military situation for some time and it was possible.

'That I cannot tell you.' The monk turned to the people. 'Does anyone know who these evil men are?'

No-one answered but there was some shaking of heads. Athyll indicated to Medrin that she dismount, then followed her.

'Well, we must believe that they are Danes,' he told the monk.

The priest now named himself as Alcine and said he had been on a pilgrimage to the Abbey of Glastonbury when he had met the refugees some miles back. He did not know where they could go from here, he told Athyll, and would be grateful for his advice.

Athyll suggested that the people rest and took Medrin to one side. 'Medrin, I think you will have to go to Winchester by yourself — do you think you could do that?'

The girl looked anxious. 'But why should I go alone? Why will you not come?'

'You heard what the monk told me — there is great danger here from a group of marauders and they must be stopped.' Medrin understood this but not how it could be done. Athyll explained that there were a number of young men among these people who would be asked to join him.

Though still doubtful, Medrin listened to the rest of his plan. She was to take the horse and go with the people on to Winchester. Once there she was to go to the Earl of Bedford and tell him what was happening in the south, and her story from the time she was ravished by Egbert until arriving back in the city. Though she had reservations at the moment about how much she would tell the Earl, she did want to see the merchant brought to justice and agreed to do as Athyll had asked.

This settled, Athyll went to Alcine and explained what he intended to do. The monk thought the plan fraught with danger but gave his blessing. After they had all rested for an hour Athyll gathered together all the available men he thought would be able to fight. There were some thirty in all but of these he could only persuade ten to join him in an attempt to stop what could be hundreds of these destroyers of people and places. He also found that the only weapons they had were an axe and a hunting bow useful but less efficient than the military type. Searching the carts Athyll found pieces of chain usually fixed to the wheel to stop it sliding downhill when heavily loaded. With these he had to be content but it was clear to him that direct contact with the other force would have to be avoided at all costs. It would be stalk and strike, then quickly vanish, he told himself grimly.

It was time for the column to move off. Medrin, at its head, did not look back. She was feeling better than she had done since she had been taken first to Winchester by Athyll and, though far from enjoying her present situation, she felt pride in herself again as she led these people to the protection of the well-defended and friendly city. Even when one woman screamed and tried to join her young husband standing with Athyll and the other men, she still did not look back. The woman was pulled back and dragged along as the motley assembly slowly made its way north.

Athyll watched the column go. He told the men what he was going to do and what would be required of them, then ordered them to rest so as to be ready to move when darkness fell.

The time soon came and, after having eaten fruit only, the small group carefully made its way westwards, keeping to the thickets and low ground in order to avoid open ground. As daylight came Athyll estimated that they had covered ten miles and was not displeased with their progress. With the exception of the young man whose wife had been distressed, all appeared to be accepting their strange situation very well — one had even ventured the opinion privately to Athyll that it was doubtful if they would meet this band of men who were said to be terrorising the area. It was true that there had been no sign of them so far but Athyll, with experience and instinct guiding him, warned that man not to judge the situation too hastily.

It was on the third night, when they had gone forty miles, that they heard the whinnying of a horse as they approached the edge of a forest. The men were in a single column behind him and Athyll signalled them to halt. He had already planned his attack — they were to approach silently and those with weapons were to kill on sight, whilst the others either fought with their bare hands or waited close by. Athyll himself intended to take one of them alive to discover who they were and their purpose.

He signalled again for the men to fan out and they moved forward on their stomachs until they came to the trees. Athyll moved first and made his way in the direction of the sound from the horse. It had stopped now so he was using his judgement; soon he came to a clearing and he saw the dim shape of a horse with a man lying down beside it. He looked round and saw two of his men close by, then slid forward until he was beside the sleeping man. Putting his hand quickly over the other's mouth, Athyll stood and dragged him several yards, stifling his attempted shouts, to where he was met by one of his men who helped carry the man until they had gone some distance.

Releasing his grip, the prisoner was about to call out when Athyll pressed the point of his sword to his neck.

'Now, who are you and what are you doing here?' he whispered in crude Norse, hoping that he would be understood. The man struggled then cried out as Athyll put his knee sharply in his groin. But the words he had used were 'Christ Almighty'. Athyll had heard enough and put the sword in the man's face.

'So that's it,' he breathed softly. 'What we have here is a Saxon traitor.' He pressed the sword to the other's cheek and drew blood. 'Now, where are you from and how many of you are there?'

In a position from which he could not move and feeling the blood running into his mouth, he spat some out. He looked up at Athyll and the two men near him. 'I am not telling you anything,' he said at last, thinking that he must have been missed by this time and his friends would be looking for him.

'No matter, there cannot be more than a few dozen of you and they can easily be dealt with,' replied Athyll calmly.

The man fell into the trap. 'There're three hundred and some will soon be here,' he replied angrily.

Athyll thought this a deliberate exaggeration — perhaps the figure was nearer two hundred but he had discovered something about the force he was dealing with.

He stood and pulled the mercenary up with him. 'If you have any prayers in you, say them now,' he told the man.

He looked at Athyll and his small band with surprise creasing his weather-beaten, toothless face but stayed silent. Then Athyll plunged his sword into the dirty tunic straight to the man's heart and he fell like a log to the ground, eyes wide with disbelief.

Now they had to leave the forest because that would be the first place to be searched after a dead body had been found. Moving as quickly as they could in the moonless night, they reached the edge of the forest and were able to go rapidly over more open ground. Before daylight they came across a farmhouse which had been stripped bare of its contents and there was no sign of any human or animal life. But it was a place for Athyll and the others to hide and rest and for him to decide on what further moves could be made. It now appeared to him to be impractical to continue to harass a force of some two hundred or more but he was satisfied that he had achieved the double objectives of finding out who these men were and diverting their attention, if only temporarily, from their attacks on unsuspecting, innocent people.

Rain fell steadily during the morning of their arrival but the group were able to find places in the crude building in which to settle, in spite of the leaking roof. The problem was food, only a few nearly-rotting vegetables were found stacked in a corner under some sacking and there was a barrel of water. Whilst they were chewing raw vegetables Athyll was able to find out more about his company. They were simple country folk, unable to read or write, who all worked on the land except the young man Elgin, who had helped his father as a mason before he had been killed.

They asked him about the King and Athyll explained Alfred's desire to serve his people and to educate them for a better life; how he was going to alter the laws so that they would serve all his subjects. The strong moral tone of the King's thought struck a chord in these men and he was pleased to give them some idea of what was happening in the country, even if they were barely able to grasp the importance of these stirring events. The mason's son was particularly keen to understand and Athyll had to answer many questions for him.

When the rain had stopped guards were mounted in the high scrub around the perimeter and late in the afternoon a horseman wearing a Norse helmet appeared, followed by a group of men carrying spears. A signal was sent back to Athyll in the building and, as they neared the place, he ran out with his sword and before the rider knew what was happening he was cut down, bringing the horse with him on to the hard ground where it stayed. Athyll lunged again and cut the man's throat. As he turned a spear was thrust at him but he jumped to one side and caught the man with a turn of the sword to his stomach.

All around him now was a melee of men fighting, lurching and swaying as they exchanged blows — some of his men fighting with their bare fists. He saw one go down with a spear in his heart and ran swinging his sword with a sideways movement which decapitated the attacker. He himself just managed to move quickly to one side as another spear came through the air at him. It hit one of the raiders and he fell to the ground. Then the rest, seeing their losses around them, turned and ran. As one of his men made to follow, Athyll called to him to let them go.

He surveyed the carnage. Of his band one had died and one was wounded; of the others there were four dead and one had received so severe a blow from the axe that he was bleeding to death. Controlling his sudden feeling of nausea Athyll ordered the man's suffering to be put to an end, then turned his attention to the horse struggling to rise from the ground. One back leg was hanging loosely and had been broken when the animal had fallen. There was nothing that could be done; one swift action from the blood-stained sword and the horse gave a last heavy sigh as it fell.

The wounded man was attended to with the best that could be done and, whilst they were sitting recovering, one of the band, a tall thin man, appeared wearing a Danish helmet with his pale blue eyes just visible through the visor. The sight was so incongruous that it set them all laughing and there were some crude comments about other uses for the helmet and suddenly the tension was relieved.

They now gathered the bodies together to build a funeral pyre but it took some time to find sufficient tinder to get round the bodies but at last steel on flint lit the spark and the bodies were soon blazing.

There was no point in staying at this place — there was nothing there; the stench of the burning bodies would soon become unbearable, and more raiders were almost certain to return. Athyll got the small band together, now less one, and told them they would have to leave.

'We have done all we can do here. You are all free to go as you please.'

There was an embarrassed silence as the men looked from one to the other, each waiting for the first to speak.

'If you wants my wishes, sir, it is to stay with you,' said Elgin, breaking the silence at last.

'Yes, and me,' said another, then another, until all had said they would follow Athyll.

'Thank you all for your trust but you have done well and there is no more purpose for us here.'

'What is you going to do now, sir?' asked one.

'I am going to try and rejoin the King's forces coming this way from Winchester.'

They had been moving in a southwesterly direction for some days since leaving the refugees, so he was sure they must be near a town and he hoped to meet the King's troops somewhere in that region.

''Us can tell from the air we'm near the coast, sir — maybe find a Danish ship and sink it,' the lean man said. He was not wearing the helmet and his hollow weather-beaten features showed only the faintest sign of a smile.

'What with — a spear or axe?' asked Elgin, laughing.

The lean one having been right about their nearness to the coast, it was the small port of Wareham into which nine weary, travel-stained men later found their way. They walked along a deserted main street until they came to the harbour — a solitary boat, a long coracle, rode the water as it lapped gently against the stout wooden wall. They waited but still there was no sign of life. Athyll called out once, twice, then a man appeared at the door of a small hut made with a wooden frame covered with thatch.

'Who is it — what d'ye want?' he shouted.

Athyll walked towards the man but he retreated back into his hovel. Not to be put off the soldier followed him in but it was dark inside — he could not see anything at first, then he noticed the two shapes crouching on the floor and another standing beside them.

'We are friends and you have nothing to fear,' he called out to what he could now see as a woman and child cowering before him. The man stepped forward and Athyll briefly explained the presence of himself and the others in the place. The man made the sign of the cross and said he was Bellan, a fisherman — the two with him were his family.

'Saints be praised — methinks them Danes come back,' he told Athyll, excusing his behaviour.

'The Danes here? — When was this?' asked Athyll, his voice calm though there was a tightening of the muscles of his stomach.

'Why, sir, 'twas six or more days since and comes in ships they did,' the man replied.

Following their usual pattern of attack after landing in different places on the coast, the Danes had terrorised the town and countryside, pillaging and burning as far inland as Sherbourne. The people of Wareham now took shelter in the local community hut for most of the time, venturing out only as necessity demanded, since no outside protection could be given to them. The force on its way from Winchester had only begun to move after the attacks had been made and the fleet which King Alfred was building to meet superior Danish ships was still not ready — those which were in service were having to defend a very long coastline.

Athyll, tired and dispirited, was now content to let events take their natural course and wait. Looking for a place to stay, he found one that was no more than a long room with a thatched roof supported by six stout poles. It was where the fish were cleaned and gutted before being taken by cart to nearby markets. It smelled, but not too unpleasantly, and the men claimed they liked it — whether this was true or simply to please him Athyll could not tell. At all events they settled in and slept the clock round on their first day in the place.

Feeling in need of exercise after waking and having a meal, Athyll went down to the harbour and saw one long fishing boat already out at sea and the other being prepared to leave.

The fisherman — it was Bellan — looked up at him and waved cheerily.

'Looking fer some fishing, sir?' he called.

Athyll hesitated. The boat did not look strong enough for two people. 'How long for?'

The man looked up at the sky, considering the weather. There were dark clouds in the southeast, moving slowly toward them. 'Two hours, maybe less.'

Having decided to take the risk, Athyll edged himself over the wall carefully into the boat. It rocked for a moment, then steadied, and soon they were headed out to sea. The other boat had disappeared behind a headland and they were now steady on the water, the man throwing out a crude net made of rough twine.

They had been there for nearly an hour and had made a reasonable catch when Athyll saw a black shape appear on the horizon. He pointed it out to the fisherman and they both watched as it seemed to be getting closer. Then the shape became a square-rigged sail attached to a mast but tied down either side of the vessel. And rising up out of the bow was the figure of a horse's head, the symbol of the Vikings.

'My God, the Danes are come,' the man shouted. He grabbed a long paddle and indicated to Athyll that he do the same. 'Sir, there's not much time 'fore they gets 'ere.'

By a supreme effort they managed to make the harbour before the Danish ship furled its sail and moved in close to the beach. From there the Danes would have to disembark and make their way from some distance to the harbour and then into the town. Athyll ran to alert his men and the fisherman to warn the people to go to the main hut or hide as best they could.

Athyll reached the long building and got his sword but the man he called the Lean One was the only one of his company there. He did not stop to ask where the rest of the men were but, signalling to the man to follow, he ran into the street. There was still no sight of the Danes and, looking round, he decided to take the path to the cliff where he would be able to watch them coming from the beach. Lean One saw his intention and suddenly ran past him at surprising speed.

They reached the top and could see about a dozen men moving swiftly and the first of them were now almost at the harbour. Lean One made for a pile of small rocks besides the path. More were at the cliff edge and Athyll lifted one and together they heaved the rocks over the cliff. They watched as one hit a Dane as he looked up when the crude missile fell. There was a scream of pain which came to them faintly and there was a yelp of delight from Athyll's companion. Now they both put their feet on a pile by the edge and two more men below were hit, but by now the leaders had reached the harbour and the first man was in the street.

There was no-one else in view until two of Athyll's men ran out of a house and one of them cut down the leading man with his axe. It was Eldon, then he fell as a spear pierced him. Athyll and Lean One ran to meet the Danish party and at the bottom of the cliff path four more of the small band of Anglo-Saxons joined in, some only carrying planks of wood or metal spikes as weapons.

Athyll rushed at a Dane and felt his sword enter the man's neck, then he felt a searing pain in his thigh as he turned to face another and a spear pierced his leg. He staggered, fell, and there was more pain as a large boot was pressed into his body as someone walked over him. Now the sky went black and got even darker, then faded away altogether as he lost consciousness.

Waking later he was in a long room and a man was bending over him. It was the local Apothecary. He had tended Athyll's wounds and now gave him something to drink which tasted like pine. He looked down at his charge and smiled. 'You will have to rest for some days, my son, but with God's help you will recover fully from your wound.'

Athyll asked about his men. He was told one had died and another, Eldon, had been wounded like himself. There had been five Danes killed in the fighting and one, taken prisoner after being injured, had been put to death after the raid in which more houses had been burned and more people killed. None could say how many Danes there had been off their ship.

The news was not bad, thought Athyll, but the raid was another sign of the vulnerability of the people of Wessex to sudden and continuous attack. But that night Athyll developed a fever and became delirious, and he did not hear the news next day that the Danish ship which had brought the raiders to Wareham had been caught in a storm and dashed to pieces against the rocks nearby.

Chapter 8

When Medrin arrived at Winchester with the motley convoy of the monk Alcine and some hundred men, women and children, they found the capital *en fête* for the investiture of Denewulf, the new Bishop. There were crowds in the street everywhere and they could not move when they came to the main road leading to the Church where the wooden tower was gaily bedecked with flags of all kinds, its bells pealing out their message for a joyous occasion.

All the refugees could do was stand and watch, confused and puzzled, with the children beginning to cry at the strangeness of the scene. Medrin, not sure what was happening, had to calm her horse as it shied at the crowds and the noise. Attracted by the sound of an animal amongst the people, a steward carrying a staff hurried to Medrin and was about to protest to her when he saw the horse with its military trappings and stopped short. He looked up at her and her haughty expression, together with the horse, associated her with someone of importance.

'What is your wish, lady?' he asked respectfully.

'To get out of this crowd. We have come a long way and want to be settled,' she told him, then added: 'And I have to see the Earl of Bedford.'

The man nodded, understanding, and caught hold of the horse's bridle. As he moved off several more people tried to join those at the roadside and he had to push them off with his staff. Slowly, with the rest of the company following in bewilderment, he led the horse through the streets until they came to a large part of open ground used as a market place and away from the dense mass of people.

'Now show me, where is the Earl of Bedford's place?' Medrin asked the man, her accent thick now with the dust in her throat and tiredness. The man did not notice — he had heard different versions of the English language that day — and told her she would have to wait for someone from the Earl's household to take her to him.

After he had gone Medrin dismounted and sat on the soft grass away from the others. She had not mixed with them very much on the journey, spending most of her time helping with the children; for the most part they had stood somewhat in awe of this tall, beautiful, and mysterious girl. Now, in spite of her outwardly calm demeanour, she was feeling nervous and unsettled about the forthcoming meeting with one of the most important men in the Kingdom of Wessex.

Looking up, she could see the Cathedral tower and wondered about the meaning and purpose of the church, never having seen one before. She did not dislike these Anglo-Saxon people since they were brave, resolute, and resourceful like her own, but they did have this strange religion and practices which she did not understand. She thought of Athyll and how religious he might be, as he had never mentioned his faith to her. Where was he now and what was he doing? Already disspirited, it distressed her even more to think that he might be fighting her people and might himself have been killed.

Her reverie was broken by the monk Alcine. 'I am going to hold a short service of thanksgiving here,' he told her. 'Will you join us, my child?'

Medrin forced herself to smile. 'No, please, I will stay here as I have to wait.'

The monk was a little displeased with the response. 'As you wish, Medrin, as you wish,' he said and returned to the others huddled together in a forlorn group.

The simple but impressive ceremony of the investiture of the Bishop of Winchester was over and a small group stood outside at the entrance to the Cathedral. They were King Alfred and the Bishop Denewulf, dressed in their different robes of office and headgear; the Earl of Bedford, and the man who had performed the service, the priest Ulban.

Alfred shook hands warmly with Denewulf and the new Bishop responded by taking the King's right hand and kissing it.

'Look upon me as I am this hour, sire, for such a moment comes only once in a man's lifetime,' said Denewulf, greatly moved by the honour which the King had given him. He had been a simple shepherd and devout

Christian working by himself when Alfred, a keen judge of men and struck by Denewulf's intelligence and humour, had taken him back to Winchester and installed him at his court with the purpose of grooming him for a position within the State such as he now held.

The King merely smiled and patted his shoulder.

'You have nothing to fear, Denewulf — time can strengthen as well as weaken,' said Bedford. He also liked the man and recognised his humility and goodness.

The horses had arrived at the courtyard and the royal party mounted to begin their triumphal journey through the city to the King's residence. Slowly the procession made its way along the packed route, the cheers and cries of the people showing their regard for Alfred and his wise rule and for the new Bishop. Flowers were thrown and strewn in their path and at one place a woman ran out and kissed the hem of the King's silk gown. He smiled and touched her head with his gloved hand and she fell to the ground weeping until she was pulled back by two people running out from the crowd.

So the royal quarters were reached and the retinue entered. But first there were matters of State to attend to and his court, then guests, had to await the King's business before the festivities began. With his usual energy Alfred dealt with every problem and question as they arose; if he could not he would pass them on to one of his courtiers or aide, otherwise he would keep the issue in mind until a suitable settlement could be found.

There were more reports of Danish raids on the south coast, a matter which had been troubling him lately, but there was also good news — nine ships had been completed at the Thames boatyard and were ready for service awaiting their crews. Other minor things were brought to his attention and an old servant told the King, with a familiarity which would not have been tolerated by a lesser man, that a messenger had news for the Thane, Lord Bedford.

Having satisfied himself about his official business, King Alfred returned to his guests. He singled out the Earl and told him he was needed to get some information which could be important. Bedford agreed and, excusing himself, went to an outhouse where he found his man drinking ale with another servant. He ordered the man to see the messenger and deal with the matter unless it was sufficiently serious to require his personal attention.

The building, though it was the King's Headquarters, was a modest one which consisted of a large main hall with bedrooms and a place for work and study leading off it. Food was prepared in an outhouse and brought over to the main hall — on this occasion the King's guests occupied every seat at his table and it was full of the best food that could be had. At its very head, seated on the King's right, was his Queen, Aelswith, and beside her was his son Edward, aged fourteen, and daughter Ethelfled, two years younger. On Alfred's left was the Bishop and the rest of those present included his army commanders Sir Galwain and Sir Edwig, and various court and city officials. There was also one man, Sir Edgar from London, who was his new adviser on ships.

As Bedford re-entered the hall, Denewulf was saying a prayer. He crossed himself and knelt until it ended and then took his place at the table. The wine was poured into the goblets and the meal began. The gathering, in spite of the steady flow of wine, was kept alert by the King's conversation. It was not that he would attempt to show a person's ignorance but they were themselves at pains to prove their knowledge. If Alfred found he was learning nothing he would simply change the person and the subject.

When the meal had ended the King announced what measures would soon be taken against Danish marauders on the coast and on the Mercian border — more ships were now ready to join the present inadequate fleet. There were cheers and Edward rose to his feet.

'Father, I want to be allowed to join the men who will sail those ships.'

There were more cheers but Alfred stayed them with his hand. 'No, my son, I cannot grant your wish. You will be King one day and your task will be to rule and lead all the forces, though, pray God, they will not be needed.'

'Amen to that, sire,' murmured Denewulf.

The Queen took Edward gently by the hand, seated him again and whispered something to him. His sister, near to tears, also had to be comforted, but now a servant came in to declare that the players were ready to start their performance. The Earl of Bedford went to the Royal couple and excused himself, saying he wished to leave before the entertainment began.

First there were the acrobats from France, who did amazing feats considering the amount of space at their disposal; then crout and harp players making music together. Finally came a singer — she was a small girl with a simple gown and head-dress. She began with a traditional air, then came a song composed by her poet father. She sang with a pure soprano voice:

This year our King, Alfred
Lord of the Jutes and Angles

CHAPTER EIGHT

Saviour of honour of men
Has won undying glory
in Warfare and Conflict;
With forged blades the sons
of Anglia have routed the
enemy cleaving shield and mail;
To defend their homes, their
treasures in battle royal
to Victory.

When the song ended it was the last of the entertainment. After collecting the money which had been donated — not too generously — the small party made to leave. Pende, a young nephew of the Queen who had been watching the singer closely, caught up with her as she reached the main doorway and took her arm. She looked up at him uncertainly, then smiled. Now arm-in-arm they left together.

Chapter 9

It was dark when Medrin awoke. She had been waiting a long time and had fallen asleep, now a hand was gently shaking her. It was a woman servant. 'Medrin, a messenger is here from my Lord Bedford,' she was saying.

Medrin sat up in confusion, having to remember what she was doing in this place and why a messenger should want to see her. She was lifted gently from the high-backed chair and as she was led from the darkened room it all came back to her.

She explained to the messenger her mission to the Earl of Bedford, but only gave him in the broadest outline the reasons for her escape from the merchant Egbert's service. The details of the actual attack on her, Medrin decided, would be saved for the man who would deal with the case.

The Earl's messenger was also in no doubt that it was a matter for his master. He had watched the girl closely whilst she had been talking, and with the mention of Athyll, a soldier in the service of the Thane, he was convinced she was telling the truth. He was also certain that he had not heard the whole story but wisely thought that it was no concern of his to question Medrin further.

'Very well. What you have told me will be conveyed to my Lord but at present he is with the King. Your meeting will have to wait until morning,' he told her, then turned to the serving woman. 'Please arrange for this girl to be given food and rest for the night and bring her here early in the morning.'

The woman nodded but Medrin had not understood the reference to the King; then she remembered that Winchester was the capital and his city. The thought pleased her in some way as she followed the woman across the yard to the servants' quarters.

71

A crude bed of straw could have been a royal couch; it was such a luxury compared to that which she had suffered lately. Nevertheless she slept fitfully and had a dream in which she was being pursued by a man but when he got near and caught her in his arms he changed suddenly to Athyll. He bent to kiss her and at first she submitted, then began to struggle and broke away from him. She started to run but the figure of Egbert stepped into her path. She turned and was caught from behind and again the figure had changed to that of a soldier — struggling in his arms she woke up, her heart beating rapidly and in a cold sweat.

She picked her way past two sleeping bodies to the door; opening it the cool air on her body refreshed and calmed her. She went back to her bed but could not sleep, then tiredness overcame her.

Medrin awoke again to the sound of a cockerel crowing but was now alone in the room. She got up and went into the yard where there was a well — she would have liked to immerse her whole body in water but she had to be satisfied with washing her face and arms. As she was drying herself with grass a voice called to her from the main building. She looked up and saw a young man walking toward her carrying something wrapped in a cloth. He came up to her and eyed her tall body, then they settled on the firm rounded shape of breasts beneath the thin woollen gown.

'Is your name Medin?' he asked abruptly.

'My name is Medrin,' she corrected him. 'What you want?'

He grinned as the question brought a fanciful thought to his mind but he answered it factually. 'I've brought food.'

He opened up the cloth. There was a greasy bit of mutton, a bit of cabbage and some bread. Medrin took it without relish and made to go back to the room. The man followed her to the door and she turned on him angrily. 'You have brought the food — now go.'

'I've been told to stay,' he said, still grinning.

'Then you stay outside,' she told him over her shoulder and slammed the door behind her.

She ate a little of the food, then waited to be called before Lord Bedford, earnestly hoping that it would not be too long. To her relief a loud knock on the door came and the woman who had been with her the previous evening appeared. A few minutes later she was standing in the large hall, which had not been prepared in any special way, and there was only one person present — the monk Orfran, clerk and translator for Lord Bedford. He greeted her politely in Norse and brought a chair for her.

CHAPTER NINE

'Ah! You are Medrin — please be seated. Lord Bedford will be here soon,' he told her.

'Thank you, but please speak in English.' Instinctively she answered in Norse but she did not want delays in translation or its possible prejudicial effect on her case. The monk nodded and went back to his table.

Lord Bedford started his questioning in a manner which indicated that he considered this meeting with Medrin an interruption of more important matters requiring his attention. He looked tired and unwell as he faced the girl and asked her to explain her reasons for what he considered an unreasonable request to see him personally.

Medrin began nervously but was determined to be heard. 'Sir, you remember that you sent me to work for Egbert the merchant. For a time it was very bad for me, then it got better — I given better work and room and was more happy. But one night the merchant came to me and he . . .' She paused and asked Orfran the English of the Norse meaning to violate a woman, then went on: 'ravished me . . .'

'Do you mean raped?' interrupted Bedford sharply.

'Yes, lord, I'm afraid she does,' Orfran replied.

'After that I became very ill but ran away, sir. That is my story but I have been told the merchant can be brought to justice,' Medrin went on quickly.

Bedford considered the girl thoughtfully. 'And who told you this?' he asked.

'The soldier, Athyll.'

'And where is this man now?'

'I do not know, sir. We met some people who said robbers made them leave their homes — he went with other men to find them.'

This tallied with what Bedford already knew, for only that morning he had had to deal with the refugees from the southwest and accommodate them and their cattle and other possessions, such as they were. But this story of rape from a girl who was, after all, a foreigner and an enemy, was a serious charge which carried the penalty of death.

'Can any other person confirm your claim, girl?' the Thane asked her. Medrin had to think to recall the girl's name. 'Yes — a servant girl at merchant's house. Her name Ellen.'

Earl Bedford sat and drummed his fingers on the table, then told Orfran to fetch a servant to him.

'Now, I am going to send for the merchant Egbert and the girl and I will hear what they have to say,' he told Medrin, 'but I wish you to stay should the merchant need to question you.'

When the servant came he was given his orders to bring the two people to him and get food for the girl and Orfran, then Bedford went away to eat elsewhere.

Medrin and the monk ate without speaking, then silence was broken by Orfran.

'Is what you are doing wise, Medrin?'

She looked up at him in surprise. 'Yes — why is it not?'

'In these matters it is best to turn to God and place oneself in His merciful hands.'

'I know nothing of this God,' she replied shortly, and went on eating.

'Then surely it is time you learned of Him, of His infinite wisdom and goodness and how He gave His only son to die for us on the Cross of Calvary.' The monk leaned across the table and took her hand. 'Place yourself in my hands, child, and let me prepare you to enter the Church of Christ the Saviour.'

Medrin thought for a moment, then asked: 'Is the merchant Egbert a man of your Church?'

'Of course — why do you ask?'

'What will your God think of him?'

'If he repents he will be forgiven — we are all sinners, Medrin, but if we are all truly repentant we shall see the Kingdom of Heaven.' The monk smiled. 'None of us has anything to fear once we embrace God's church and accept His word.'

Medrin did not understand the reasoning — her moral thinking was more basic and simple. 'What is right and wrong is here,' she said, pointing to her head. 'It is that which tells us we have to answer.'

Now she wanted to get away from the subject and the man. She rose from the table, pointedly turning her back on him, and walked away. She moved round the room, studying different objects with exaggerated concern. She was at the table and had her back to the door when the Earl of Bedford returned, followed by Egbert. When she heard the door close and their steps behind her she turned and faced the merchant across the room. Her instinct was to run to him and pummel him with her fists but she resisted it and was the first to turn away.

74

CHAPTER NINE

Bedford made them stand at the table, some distance apart, and took his seat in front of them. He turned to Medrin.

'Now that the merchant is here, girl, I want you to make your accusations directly to him.'

Medrin did so and was angered to see a smile playing on his lips as she spoke, haltingly at first then gaining confidence as she could see the Thane watching the man's reaction closely. When she had told the story for the second time, Bedford sat back in his chair.

'Well, sir, you have heard the girl — what have you to say?'

The merchant spread his hands in supplication. 'My lord, I strongly deny these allegations — there is not a word of truth in them. I must ask you, for the sake of my good name in this city, and of my family, to dismiss the matter for the falsehood that it is.'

Medrin turned to the monk and spoke rapidly to him. He replied and she went back to Lord Bedford.

'Ask him to bare his wounds to you,' she almost shouted at him. Bedford indicated that the man do so. He hesitated and looked from one person to another, not knowing what to say or do.

'My lord, this is a monstrous suggestion,' he said, breathing fast. 'How can you listen to this girl, this — enemy . . .'

Bedford stared hard at the man. 'Do as I say, merchant — if you have nothing to hide no harm will have been done,' he said, quietly but firmly.

Slowly Egbert removed his light cloak, then his top garment, leaving him standing in breeches. Lord Bedford had no need to rise from his chair and look — from where he sat the wounds could be plainly seen. There was a hole in the upper part of the body and below this was a gash at least four inches in length; in his left side was another gash indicating a knife wound.

'So the girl was right,' said Bedford, 'even to placing the wounds.'

'But they were not made by her, I promise you — they were made by two men who attacked me in the street one night.'

'Then how came she to know about them?'

'It was common knowledge the next day,' answered the merchant, now feeling on safer ground, then added: 'The girl was still with my household then, my lord.'

'The servant Ellen can say that I was not — I ran away the same night,' replied Medrin coldly, calmer now.

'Yes, the girl Ellen,' Bedford repeated thoughtfully, recalling her role in the affair. 'She is not with you now, merchant — when did she leave and where did she go?'

Egbert had dressed and was nervously scratching the back of his hand. 'Oh, it was some weeks ago,' he lied, 'and I do not know where she went.' He was about to add that she had not been a good servant but thought better of it.

'Then she must be found . . .'

'And the soldier Athyll — he is my witness also,' put in Medrin quickly.

'Yes, yes, a messenger has already been sent — he is needed here for military duties,' Bedford replied impatiently. He turned to Egbert. 'As for you, sir, you will be held for trial by jury of the Witan. I would remind you that the crimes of rape and perjury both bring death by hanging — I would strongly recommend you to make peace with your Maker before it is too late!'

Bedford stood, swayed slightly, then fell forward. He saved himself by placing his hands on the table. Orfran ran toward him and placed a strong arm round his shoulders. Bedford pushed the monk roughly away.

'I am all right, Orfran.' He paused and straightened himself. 'Now — you know what you have to do, man. See to it straight away.'

Orfran nodded and with a muttered 'Of course, my lord,' went and stood by the trembling merchant. The action was meant to deter a false move but, whilst Egbert was considering how he could get away, two armed soldiers entered and led him away. Medrin was wondering what she should do when the question was answered for her. The woman who appeared to have been assigned to her came in and the girl was led back to a building where several female servants were sitting talking or were engaged on simple household tasks such as repairing clothes and linen. And now the Dane welcomed their company with relief, almost pleasure.

At the insistence of Bedford the search for Ellen, the servant girl, was to be immediate and very thorough. It began at the house of Egbert, where it was discovered that she had left just a week after she had helped Medrin to get away from the place. The search was then extended to the home of her parents, where it was found that her father had died suddenly and her mother had been taken by Ellen to Ockley, a village some fifty miles to the east of Winchester, to stay with a sister. This done, she had said that she was going back to the capital to find work.

Fortunately for the Thane's men who were doing the searching, there were not many outlets for the employment of a young servant girl, even for one of Ellen's skill as a dressmaker and a quick learner of everything to which she put her mind and hand. However, the people of Wessex born and bred were reluctant to give details about their fellow men and women and it took much time and diligent work to trace the girl. Eventually she was traced to a weaver's hut, where she worked on the loom and carried out repairs to dresses and soldiers' clothing.

She was in the hut attending the loom when Bedford's two attendants called and said they wanted to see her. She looked anxiously at the other women in the hut, and the weaver's wife, in answer to her unspoken question, told her to carry on working.

'The girl is working — what does 'ee want with her?' the woman told the men as she nervously picked off pieces of fluff from her gown.

'We are the Thane's men — just bring her to us,' said one impatiently. He had had enough of this task, believing it beneath his dignity as a public servant, and wanted to get it finished. His companion, less concerned with his social position, was looking at the girl and admiring her dark brown hair, her smooth skin and clear brown eyes, her slim, rounded body. He was thinking she must have some Celtic blood in her and those people were said to be of a passionate nature.

'If us stops loom now 'twill spoil the weave,' complained the woman.

'Very well, we will wait,' put in the second, younger man, and, at a hard look from his companion, added: 'but be quick — we have little time to spare.'

The first man went outside the small hut but the other stayed, his eyes still on the girl. At a sharp word from the woman she carried on until the piece of cloth she was working on was finished. She got up from her stool and made her way to the man standing at the opening, carefully avoiding his gaze. As she came by him he placed his hand on her thin gown and felt the top of her thigh. She pushed it away and brought her hand sharply across his face. The man was not put out but simply smiled — her reaction merely confirmed the first impression he had of the girl.

The men explained to her that she was needed as a witness in the trial of her previous employer for the attack on Medrin and that she was to be taken to swear a statement before the monk Orfran. Ellen was not pleased with the news but she wanted to know more about Medrin.

'Is she well now?'

'Yes, she is — but we must leave,' said the young man impatiently.

But now Ellen was thinking of the young soldier who had gone to search for the Danish girl, perhaps at risk to himself. 'And Athyll — the soldier — what happened to him?'

The men protested they knew nothing about a man called Athyll, and hustled her away to make the two-mile journey on foot to the Earl of Bedford's residence in the centre of the city.

The taking of the statement took some time. Orfran was a meticulous man and scripted her words laboriously and slowly. He would frequently stop to question the girl, or get her to repeat what she had said so as to clarify a point or test her truthfulness. In addition, the girl's nearness was disturbing him. In fact, Orfran the monk was seriously beginning to doubt the wisdom of having taken to the cloth, though he knew that not all his brethren felt inhibited when their natural instinct was urging them to follow its course.

At last the business was finished and beads of sweat were standing out on the man's forehead. To add to the discomfort the girl did not seem anxious to leave.

'Please, Father, do you know what has happened to Athyll the soldier?' she asked nervously, but quite unaware of the effect she was having on the monk.

He wiped his forehead with the sleeve of his habit, somewhat relieved now. 'Yes — as far as I am aware he is somewhere southwest in the country and attempts are being made to find him.' The sweat was rising again. 'He is needed to appear with you as witness to this dreadful happening,' he added in an undertone, then quickly gathered up his papers. Excusing himself he hurriedly moved off.

Ellen went the long walk back to the hut, where she slept as well as worked, in pensive mood, her thoughts on Athyll. She stopped at one point to lay down beside the path and daydream; consequently it was late. When she eventually arrived, the woman scolded Ellen and beat her about the ears.

'That's giving ee what my husband 'as just given me for lettin' ee go,' she gasped, ignoring the fact that the girl had had no choice in the matter and that she had not given her husband any explanation. Indeed, being a hard-working man, who had to tend his sheep for wool and also cultivate a small plot of land, he was not one to waste time listening to excuses for what he considered slackness in others, particularly when he gave them food and lodging, such as it was. But Ellen had not felt the blows and was not listening. The woman saw the girl's strange expression and became alarmed.

'I'm sorry, girl, but that man does drive me, he does,' she said and put her arm round Ellen's shoulders. The girl jerked herself free. 'It's all right — don't fret,' she snapped and ran into the hut.

The messenger who had been sent to try and locate Athyll soon tired of the task. Not only was it difficult to find one person in an area of thousands of square miles but there was danger as well. After some days' search he decided that the task was hopeless and, being close to where his sister and her husband were conveniently placed, he made his way there.

Athyll's wounds had proved to be more serious than the Apothecary had realised. After some days of delirium he was moved by cart from Wareham, first to Wimborne for more dressings and rest, then to Shaftesbury where military and other wounded from recent Danish raids were being cared for in the church of St. Ethelreda. By the time he arrived Athyll was weak and still had some fever but the wounds were slowly beginning to heal. He was bored and chafed at the enforced immobility but realised that his cure lay mainly with himself. He had been told of ancient herbal cures by his mother and used these to some effect — the rest was simply a matter of a strong constitution and time overcoming his disability.

He had been two weeks at Shaftesbury when a troop of four soldiers from Bedford's force found him. They had the foresight to bring Surgel with them and, after first feigning disinterest, the horse bolted up the roadway and back again with sheer joy at being reunited with Athyll.

Even though his condition had improved considerably, Athyll was not able to return to Winchester as he had been ordered. The four men decided to make the best of their time in the place by activities which would not have been unpleasing to the Danes. They spent the greater part of the day hunting, the rest was occupied in the search for sources of ale and suitable female company for the evening.

Athyll did not accompany them at first but went out on Surgel by himself. Later, when he told them he thought he was fit to travel, he was persuaded, against his better judgment, to go with the others to a farmhouse where they had arranged a farewell gathering for him. He was not surprised to find there were several girls there and a few men; he had been told what was expected of him during the course of the evening.

The next morning they set off for Winchester, Athyll wishing to get there as quickly as possible but the others apparently now in no great hurry. A compromise was reached whereby they would stop only once and so they proceeded, estimating their arrival in the city in two days after leaving Shaftesbury.

Chapter 10

The Earl of Bedford knew he was a dying man. As one of the King's closest and most trusted advisers, his duties had become more onerous lately and now his heart was failing him. The case of the Danish girl irked him particularly, since it concerned serious accusations against an important person in the capital and a public trial. The fact that the girl was an enemy added to his burden — though rape and such happenings were common when peoples were at war, this one could not be ignored because of the unusual circumstances which were involved.

He had yet to see the King about calling the Witan to conduct the trial — he had been putting it off for as long as possible, knowing that it would be an unpleasant meeting for both himself and King Alfred. Reluctantly, he at last made his way slowly to the new, bigger palace recently occupied by the King and his staff and asked for an audience.

Alfred was with Sir Edgar, his shipbuilder, and they were considering problems which had arisen with the new ships recently involved in actions with some from the Danish fleet. They had been built to be larger and faster than the Viking ships, but it was found that in tidal estuaries off the eastern and southern coast of England the increase in draught which accompanied the bigger ships was sometimes a disadvantage, particularly when the vessels were manned by inexperienced sailors. Sir Edgar, whilst admitting that there were problems connected with the draught, insisted that these could be overcome by the use of more skilful sailors, such as the Frisians — the seafaring people from the northwest coast of Germany who had settled in England three centuries before and were noted for their knowledge of the vagaries of the North Sea and England Channel.

The King was not convinced that this was the complete answer to the difficulties of the new fleet and a somewhat strained relationship now existed between the two men. But in spite of the urgency of getting some resolution to these vital questions affecting the security of his people, Bedford was admitted immediately and welcomed by the King. As he grasped the Thane's hand he saw the ashen, drawn look on the man's face and expressed concern.

'I am well enough, but I have a matter which demands your attention.'

Alfred saw him sway slightly then quickly supported him and led him to a chair. He seated himself and indicated that Sir Edgar do so. 'What is it, my friend? Your manner tells me that your news is not good,' he said, after considering his visitor carefully.

'Indeed, it is a matter of great urgency, sire, or I would not have sought you at this time,' Bedford answered slowly. The pain in his chest was sharp now. The King nodded, indicating that he should continue. The man caught his breath, then went on to tell Alfred of the events concerning the Danish girl. At the conclusion he paused to wipe the sweat from his forehead, then went on: 'I ask that the trial of the merchant be set as quickly as possible.'

The King had been listening attentively, now he got up and paced the floor, then turned to Bedford.

'Heaven preserve us, Bedford, do you know who this girl is?'

'Yes, indeed. According to Athyll, the soldier who took her captive, she is a woman who joined a Danish force posing as a man.' He paused. 'A disreputable business, but that is no defence to her rape by the merchant.'

'Most certainly not,' replied Alfred quickly, 'but what concerns me is that she appears to be the girl related to Guthrum and at our last meeting I promised him that she would be returned to him.' The King paused and took his seat again. 'Now, I wonder why she has made no mention of Guthrum?'

Bedford managed a grim smile. 'I am not surprised, sire. She is a woman of some character and self-reliance — I doubt that she would have called his name to shield herself.'

The King, never inactive for very long, jumped to his feet again. 'Very well, the trial must be held. Bedford, you will see my Clerk and he will attend to the matter.' He paused and came over to his friend and placed a hand on his shoulder. 'And you must then go home and rest — I will send my Apothecary to see you.'

Bedford rose slowly, grasped Alfred's hand firmly and thanked him but forbore to say that not much could be done for him. The King turned to Sir

Edgar, who had been quietly taking a mental note of what had been said and was thinking that the Danish girl ought to be placed on trial as an infiltrator of Saxon defences.

'Sir Edgar, as you have heard I will not be able to go with you to London so make your way alone and I will join you there as soon as it is possible.' He paused. 'And please bear in mind what I have said — those ships must be made more capable as weapons against Danish invasion forces.'

Sir Edgar rose and bowed stiffly. 'It is my duty and it shall be carried out.' He turned to Bedford and extended his hand. 'God be with you, my lord,' he said curtly and quickly left.

The King watched him go, a faint smile on his lips. 'A worthy man but one to take offence too quickly,' he told Bedford. The two men spoke on other matters, particularly about the activities of the Danish army in Mercia and at Gloucester, then the Thane made his way to find Orfran and give him his instructions. As he walked slowly across the courtyard he reminded himself that Athyll, the important witness to the case, had still to be found. He was hoping that the man would appear by the time of the trial — if not, he thought grimly, it would proceed without him.

The calling of the Witan came at a time for Orfran the clerk when he was being increasingly beset with desires which his monastic vows denied him. This was causing pangs of conscience; his commitment to the service of God warned him against what was carnal and sinful. Now he was torn between the two antagonistic longings and he was in a state of troubled indecision, so he welcomed the call to a period of strenuous activity.

As its composition was flexible it was decided, with the King's approval, to call no more than thirty people to judge Egbert. These were to consist of Bedford, two Bishops — young Denewulf and Elstan of Sherbourne — and the rest made up from the local landowners and sheriffs who were available to serve. The King himself, once the assembly had been called in his name and he was satisfied with its composition, decided not to attend personally but his Queen, Aelswith, was to be there in her own right.

So it was that on the appointed day Egbert was brought before the mobile court assembled in the King's palace to try him. Earl Bedford, who had been saving his strength for this day, was seated at the centre of a table arranged in a half-circle with the Queen on his right. Egbert stood in the middle of the room, the last persons at the table were seated immediately to his left and right. He was pale, thin, and nervously clasping his hands.

The Earl took up a sheet of parchment and read the charges against Egbert. Medrin sat on a high-backed chair at the back of the room, calm and composed as she heard the offences being read, but her hatred of the merchant more pronounced than ever.

Bedford looked up from the paper and asked the man for his plea.

Egbert licked his dry lips then, in a loud and clear voice, called out: 'Madame my Queen, my lord, members of this court, I swear before God that I am not guilty of these monstrous charges brought against me by this girl, this servant.' In spite of his bravado and his attempt to put a bold face on this serious situation, this last statement was a mistake. Both the Queen and Bedford knew that Medrin was of high birth and that most people, including the merchant, must have sensed this. She was certainly not of the same type as his other servants who cleaned and fetched and carried.

Orfran rose and called Medrin, asking her if she wished to speak in Norse and have it translated.

'No,' responded Medrin firmly, 'I wish to speak in English.' She came forward to take the place left by Egbert and told her story. How she had slowly improved her position at the merchant's house until she had been given her own room, then that visit from the man on a night never to be forgotten. Whilst she did not go into great detail, she left no doubt in the minds of her listeners as to the injury and humiliation she had suffered, and her reaction to both.

Bedford invited questions from the assembly. Alwain, a sheriff from Andresweald in the New Forest, rose slowly from his chair. 'Medrin, you were a virgin at this time?' he asked. He prided himself on being the Devil's Advocate.

'My Lord Bedford, I see no purpose in this question,' the Queen interposed sharply.

He nodded his agreement. 'Neither do I, madame.' He turned to Medrin. 'You need not answer that question.'

'My lord, I was simply seeking to find out if there had been some consent,' Alwain told him, but addressing the gathering.

'And I say that is untrue,' Medrin called out angrily. Then, more calmly: 'I served with the soldiers as a man and was treated so.'

Alwain looked away in some embarrassment and there was a sudden silence. The notion that a young and beautiful girl had been living with men

CHAPTER TEN

as a soldier had not been totally accepted by all of those present at this court. Some would have liked to have questioned its propriety, in spite of its irrelevance to the case. Now Bedford rose to warn that it was not the girl who was on trial but the merchant. Bishop Elstan vigorously nodded his agreement, followed by others.

Orfran called Elsa, wife of Egbert, as his witness, explaining that the two men whose names had been given him had not been traced.

Egbert quickly stepped forward. 'Majesty, my lord, they were fellow merchants passing through the city — I could only give their names and the place they said they came from,' he called out, trying to keep his voice calm but loud enough to be heard.

Bedford waved him back. 'Sir, you will have time to speak and even question but that is not now.'

Egbert was about to speak again when he caught the displeased expression of the Queen's face. He returned to his place at the back of the hall, wiping the sweat from his face.

Elsa, the small, plump woman with the blotchy features, richly dressed, gave him a nervous glance as she moved forward to face the court. She recounted how her husband had come home on that fateful night seriously wounded after being attacked by footpads. She was describing his injuries in detail when she was interrupted by Oswald, another sheriff.

'Did your husband say where he had been before he was attacked?'

The woman paused, then answered: 'Yes, sir, he said he had met two merchants and had been talking to them,' another pause, 'in the ale-house.'

'Did he name these men?'

The woman looked around her with a small birdlike movement, a worried frown on her face. 'Yes, sir, but I cannot recall them,' she replied at last in a low voice that was barely audible.

'You say the wounds that Egbert suffered were severe cuts — what weapon was used?' asked the Queen.

There was no hesitation now. 'It was a dagger, madam,' Elsa answered quickly. The Earl exchanged glances with the Queen. It had been a dagger which Medrin had said she had used to defend herself, so Egbert, if guilty, had covered his tracks carefully.

'Are you certain of that?' he asked the woman, not unkindly. He felt some pity for her because of the humiliation she was being subjected to for her husband's sake.

'Yes, I am sure of it,' she answered clearly and confidently for the first time.

Ellen, waiting anxiously in another room close to the hall, was expecting Athyll to appear at any moment and was tense with an inner excitement she was unable to control in anticipation of seeing him once again. For months he had been in her thoughts almost constantly and his absence had become something of a burden.

She had no idea how she might meet him again, if ever, until she had been told that as well as herself he would be required to give evidence when Egbert appeared before the Witan. This was the opportunity she had been waiting for these intolerably long months since she had last seen him.

There was still no sign of him when Ellen was called into the large hall. She entered, simply but well-dressed in a grey woollen gown tied in the middle with a white cord and a headdress she had made herself from pieces of blue cloth. She exchanged a shy smile with Medrin as she passed her seated by the rear wall, then stood before the imposing semi-circle of people seated round the table — a small, straight figure, slightly nervous but not overawed.

She gave her account of the events in which she had been involved in a clear voice with its barely noticeable Wessex accent. Her intelligence and service with the rich, well-educated gentry had given her a bearing and speech which merited a respect not usually given to people of her class. At first she did not dwell on the exact nature of Medrin's physical state after her ordeal but, under questioning, she did have to describe it in detail.

The Queen leaned across to the Thane sitting beside her and quietly told him, as the presider of the Court, that such injuries appeared consistent with a man having taken the girl by force. He was about to reply, in similar tone, that the question to decide was whether Egbert was the man but forbore to do so. He was thinking that the Queen's view would, at least, effectively answer an earlier question which suggested that, as Ellen had not seen the actual offence taking place, she could not know, with certainty, that it had been rape.

Ellen ended her testimony by recounting how she told Athyll, the soldier who had brought Medrin to Winchester, all that had happened to her and how he had said he would go in search of her because he had felt some responsibility for her.

Now that Egbert had the opportunity to put in a final word for himself, he seized on a last desperate attempt to sway the Court.

CHAPTER TEN

'Majesty, my lord, gentlemen of this Witan, I plead with you not to believe these vile tales that have been told against me. I have said I am innocent of these charges but would suggest that you look elsewhere for the guilty party. I suggest that the soldier Athyll had the will and the opportunity to take advantage of the girl Medrin,' he paused, 'not for the first time,' he added quickly, then went on: 'is it not strange that he is not here today? I beg of you seriously to consider this and my place in this city of ours, and how I have served it faithfully and well for many years.' He paused again to let this take effect, then shouted for all to hear: 'Before my Maker, I am not guilty.'

As soon as he finished Orfran jumped up, holding his sheaf of papers. 'May I say to you, Madame, and the court, that I was about to point out that all attempts to trace the soldier Athyll have so far failed. A small force has gone to the southwest to find him and bring him to Winchester but there is no doubt it is his military duties which have detained him, and no other reason.' He sat down again, throwing the papers on the table, angry with himself for not having made this point before.

Bedford made as if to stand, then sat back as the pain caught him sharply. He waited for a moment to get his breath, the Queen looking anxiously at him as he did so. At last he held up his hand to get everybody's attention.

'My Queen — all of you — you have heard what there is to hear,' he began slowly, 'but I would emphasise two things before we consider our verdict. Firstly, that the soldier Athyll has an excellent personal record and, according to witnesses, has recently been engaged with mercenaries. Secondly, that the injuries to the girl Medrin were consistent with the act of rape as she described them.'

Ellen slowly made her way from the hall, worried and torn by doubt about Athyll and his safety. She was closely followed by Medrin who suddenly caught her by the shoulders, turned her round and faced her with a warm smile. Then she saw the strained look on the girl's face and embraced her. After a moment, in which Ellen's tears started to flow, she stepped back and held the girl from her.

'Ellen, what is it — why the tears? Everything is going well and this man will be made to pay.'

Ellen looked up and quickly dabbed her eyes with a cloth she took from her sleeve. The case of the merchant was the last thing she had on her mind and as she saw the brightness and vivacity in Medrin she was surprised that she could appear so cheerful. Apart from the trial, was she not concerned about Athyll? She did not appear to be and Ellen was about to ask Medrin the question when a sudden shyness overcame her and she stopped herself. Instead she smiled wanly and said: 'I am all right — just a little tired, that is all.' It was all she could think of saying at the moment but, after this initial encounter, the two women talked in an easy and friendly way.

In answer to a question from Ellen, the Danish girl was telling her that she did not know what she was going to do after the trial. She was about to add that she hoped to be reunited with her people when she was interrupted by the Queen. She had stated her view of Egbert's guilt to the other members of the Witan and had left immediately to seek Medrin. Ellen bowed to the Queen and with a hasty backward glance at the Dane she left them alone together.

The Queen put her arm round the girl's shoulders and led her towards her own apartment. As they slowly made their way the Queen was saying: 'Now that this dreadful business is over, Medrin, it is our wish that you be returned to your uncle Guthrum as soon as possible. Tomorrow you will leave with an escort of four men and a female servant, then travel to the Mercian border near Gloucester — there you will be handed over to your own people.' The Queen stopped and turned and faced the girl. Medrin's body was trembling with suppressed excitement and her eyes were shining. The Queen smiled at her but would have been somewhat shocked if she had known the Danish girl's feelings at that moment. She was experiencing the thrill once again, of joyous festivals and homage paid to their pagan gods by her own people when celebration was needed, and she could sense the magic and intensity of the approaching long winter nights. She was smiling as the Queen considered her, then took her arm.

'I can see I have no need to ask how you feel about returning home,' she said as she led the way up to the room that had been reserved for her in the palace, albeit for one night. Medrin's reply was just a brisk nod of her head.

In spite of the comfort which had been provided for her, Medrin spent a restless night. It was during a period of awareness that her thoughts were of Athyll. So much had been happening recently that her attention had been taken up with other things. Though Athyll had not been at the trial to give evidence, the case against the merchant had been so overwhelming that his testimony had fortunately not been necessary. Medrin had still expected to see him before she left to join her Uncle, then had come the news that she was to leave Winchester without any delay now that the trial was over.

In the stillness of the night and with her mind sharp and clear, she wondered if he was safe and well and there was regret that she would not see him before she left Wessex.

Eventually Medrin fell into a restful sleep and after two hours she awoke refreshed and free from all doubts. After a bath attended by a royal servant she dressed slowly in the new silk underwear and a brocade gown and headdress, revelling in the unaccustomed feeling of luxury. Perversely, she was now totally feminine and all thought of soldiering furthest from her mind.

She ate little breakfast and had to wait for her escort to arrive. Some time later they appeared: four soldiers of the King's personal guard, fully equipped, and a middle-aged woman, thin-featured, with alert eyes which took in everything at a glance. She sat her horse well and dismounted to assist Medrin on to the horse provided for her. Medrin eyed the side-saddle uncertainly, never having used one before. The woman Emma explained it to her and helped her to mount.

'Be careful, my lady, and treat the horse well — she is a present from the Queen to replace your own that was sent to market for sale,' she told the girl when she was safely in the saddle. Indeed, this was Aelswith's way of wishing her farewell and it dispensed with a departure which could have been embarrassing.

'Please see that she gets my thanks,' Medrin replied, then added, as the words came to her, 'I am very grateful.'

The woman nodded. 'She also asked me to tell you that the merchant had been found guilty and will hang,' Emma said, her satisfaction with the verdict and penalty plainly evident.

The party set off slowly through the city — though it was still early in the morning, street traders were already at work and women were out seeking the cheapest foodstuffs and goods. Once outside the confines of buildings and bustle of people Medrin urged her escort to greater speed and did not look back.

Egbert's execution had been set to take place three days after the trial. Bishop Denewulf, although he had been a member of the Witan which had sentenced the man to death, had struggled with his conscience ever since. He was opposed to the death penalty, except in the case of treason, because of a basic Christian belief in the sanctity of human life. He was a small man, devout but with humour, and he found the duties of his office very different from that of a humble shepherd, but tackled them with wisdom and enthusiasm. The King had been pleased with his work and a close relationship had grown between them. So, having made his decision after much heart-searching, Denewulf went to see Alfred the day before the public hanging of Egbert was to take place.

He was always certain of a hearing from the King and was admitted without much delay to his presence. Alfred had only recently returned from London and looked tired but greeted Denewulf warmly. They sat opposite each other, Alfred waiting patiently for his friend to speak. He could see that the man was distressed.

'Sire, I have come about the man Egbert,' Denewulf began. The King nodded, inviting him to continue. 'Fortunately I have not had occasion to consult you before on a matter like this but I must say that my faith tells me it is wrong to take this man's life.' He paused again but still the man said nothing. Denewulf stood and clasped his hands. 'I have come to ask that you grant mercy for this man, sire, to save his life but instead to let him be imprisoned for his offence, vile as it was.'

The King considered the man carefully. What he was suggesting would not only be unpopular but was also against his own wishes. He did not know if Guthrum was aware of his niece's violation but it would be undesirable politically should he discover it and learn that the man responsible had been saved from the gallows.

'My friend, I cannot accede to your request for very good reasons,' Alfred began. Denewulf sat again and was about to speak when the King raised his hand to stop him. 'It is the law of the land, Denewulf, and I have no intention of interfering with it in this case. Again, I have been told that great feeling has been aroused among my people — I will not go against their wishes.'

'But the man has since confessed that he had been drinking heavily and it was the wine that drove him.' To Denewulf this had been a crucial factor which had decided him to make his approach to the King.

'The thought must have been there before the wine,' replied Alfred shortly.

From his impatience Denewulf now understood that his plea had failed but he still wanted to justify it. He stood and bowed. 'I am sorry to have troubled you, sire. My thought was that the penalty was in this case too great for the man to pay. Had he lived he would have had the crime on his Christian conscience for the rest of his time but he would also have been able to make his peace with God.'

'That he may still do — but quickly.' The King went to Denewulf, took his arm and led him to the door. 'Many lives are forfeit, Denewulf, but for more worthy causes. I have lost many good men since I became King — this man Egbert is but a victim of his own terrible misdeed.' They had reached the door and Alfred shook the young man's hand. 'Now, sir, I have much to do.' The formal address was a polite dismissal. The King returned to his seat. 'Now please call on my Lord Bedford — he is a dying man and has more need of you,' he said.

Chapter 11

Athyll arrived at Winchester with his companions two hours before Egbert was to be hanged in the City's market square. It was early morning and the men were already completing the preparations by putting the rope in place and erecting barriers to keep back the crowds which always assembled. An important purpose for making the execution public was to deter others from committing capital offences — such as rape — by showing it to everybody in all its awful detail.

Athyll pulled his horse and held his hand up for the others to stop. He had a suspicion as to who the person might be who was to receive the rope round his neck. But he had to be sure.

'Who is the scaffold for?' he asked of a bearded man whose surly expression indicated that he was always being put upon to do the unpleasant tasks. He was helping to lift a tree trunk on to its supports and slowly looked up, about to give an offensive reply. Then he saw five mounted soldiers in their military finery but travel-stained and looking none too pleased.

''Tis for the merchant, Master Egbert,' he said at last and turned back to his task.

Athyll's suspicion having proved correct, he now had to find Medrin. He had intended to do so soon after arriving at Winchester but now it was urgent that he find her immediately.

He turned Surgel away from the crowd barriers and faced his party. 'Thank you, men, for your help. I find I have a call to make so I will leave you here.'

Without waiting for any reply he spurred the horse forward. The person most able to give him any information on Medrin's affairs would be Lord

Bedford so he quickly made his way there. Lady Bedford was cutting roses as he turned into the courtyard. She did not look up as his horse approached her. He dismounted but she continued to gather the flowers carefully and place them in a basket. They were yellow, with an alluring scent, the Earl's favourite flower.

Athyll hesitated until, satisfied that she had enough roses, she turned and considered him, trying to recognise him.

'I am Athyll, my lady,' he told her, answering the unasked question.

'Ah, yes, of course.' Her manner appeared distracted as she was still trying to remember. She was certainly a different Lady Bedford from the one he had last met. Athyll sensed that something was wrong and waited.

'Yes, I recall you now — you were the young man who took the Danish girl captive.'

Athyll nodded. 'Yes, Lady Bedford — I am that man.' He paused. 'It is Medrin I have come to see Lord Bedford about,' he added, not wanting to involve her. Lady Bedford looked up at him in surprise.

'The Dane, sir? What is there to discuss?'

Athyll hesitated. 'I would rather say what I have to say to your husband, my lady.'

'I'm afraid that is not possible,' she replied firmly, with some of her old authority. 'In fact, sir, my lord is dying and can see no-one.'

Athyll stared at the woman in shocked surprise. Earl Bedford was still a comparatively young man and he had not known that his commander had been taken ill.

'I'm sorry, Lady Bedford — this is sad news that I did not expect to hear.'

She nodded, understanding, then turned and made her way to the house. 'Come with me,' she called. Inside she indicated that he wait and she went alone into the room where her husband lay. He appeared to be asleep, his face turned to the wall. She went to touch him. As she did so his head rolled back and his eyes stared unseeingly at her. She closed them slowly and carefully, took a rose from the basket, and placed it in the man's hand, then joined the other to it. Methodically, she removed some dead flowers from an earthenware jar on a small table and filled it again with roses from the basket.

Athyll was still waiting anxiously when she returned to the hall. Her expression told him nothing, now set in the familiar stern line.

Then: 'Lord Bedford is dead,' she said, as much to herself as to the man standing beside her. Athyll remained silent. There were no words which could have adequately expressed his feelings at that moment. Lady Bedford, not expecting any reply from the soldier who had served her husband, made to go to her own apartment. Athyll followed her.

'Lady Bedford, the girl Medrin?' he asked as he came up beside her. She stopped and swung round on him. 'Yes, sir, what about her, this enemy person?'

At this harsh attitude Athyll hesitated for a moment but he had to see Medrin. 'I understand that the trial of Egbert is over and I want to speak to her,' he said firmly. Lady Bedford considered him carefully and her expression softened.

'Yes, I think you had that right.' She paused. Athyll suddenly sensed what was to come. 'But it is impossible, Athyll — she returned to her Uncle Guthrum by order of the King.' Her eyes left his face as she saw the distress there. 'Now, I must go — I have much to do,' she said and turned and left him.

He stood for a moment, trying to adjust his thoughts to what he had just heard. Now you will never see her again, the reality of the situation told him. But a part of him still refused to believe and accept that was how it was to be.

He left the Bedford manor in an uncharacteristically bad mood. To add to his displeasure the first person he met entering the camp site was Black Edward. He was carrying a large loaf of bread and some meat. Athyll, not trusting himself to speak to the man at this time, urged Surgel forward and tried to pass him. But the big archer stood firmly in his path, hardly having to look up at the mounted officer as from his great height he reached over the top of the horse's head.

'Sir,' he began, before Athyll could speak. 'We'm heard tell us'll be moving in the morning time. Is that true, sir?'

'I have heard nothing of this,' Athyll replied shortly. He did not want to explain that he had been away some weeks, or talk at all to the man. He suddenly dug his heels in Surgel's side and the horse moved forward instantly. His hoof came down on Black Edward's foot and the man gave a yell and jumped back as the horse trotted on. Athyll did not see the silent expletive mouthed by the archer and carried on to the stables.

Having handed Surgel over to a groom he discovered from a fellow cavalryman that the present Commander of the camp was Aldan of Ellandun, the grizzled, ageing but still active cavalry officer who had recently been promoted and whose main responsibility was the training of both cavalry and foot soldiers.

After some searching Athyll found the man inspecting some equipment with which, by the look on his face, he was clearly dissatisfied. He hissed something into the ear of the man standing beside him and thrust a bridle and saddle into his hand. As he turned he came face to face with Athyll. He looked hard at him for a moment.

'Athyll of York, I take it,' he said at last. The young man nodded. 'Good, I have been expecting you.' Without another word he made his way to a small pinewood building. This served as his centre of operations and sleeping quarters — a small table was littered with papers, mostly maps, and there was a wooden bed squeezed into one corner.

Aldan did not believe in wasting time. 'Now, I will assign you to a section of horse and marching men,' he told Athyll who had followed him. He went on to explain the reason for this unusual grouping and eventually sat on the edge of the table. 'We have mostly tented places here but I am giving you a hut to share with two other men.' He turned and sorted out a sheet of paper and handed it to Athyll. 'This is a list of men you will command — see that you get them together by the morning when the whole camp is assembled.'

Athyll took the paper and put it in the top of his boot without looking at it. 'Yes, sir.' He paused.

'Was there something else you need to know?' asked Aldan.

'No, sir, but I thought you should be aware that the Earl of Bedford is dead.'

'You know this to be sure?'

Athyll resented the implication of the question. 'I have come from his place and was told so by Lady Bedford herself,' he snapped.

Aldan crossed himself quickly. 'So be it — may God rest his soul.'

Then, as Athyll was still waiting: 'Thank you — now see to your duties.'

After he had found his hut Athyll looked at his list and saw a name that he recognised and trusted. It was an archer, Harald, who had served in Mercia and East Anglia. The rest of the men on the list were unknown to him so he went to the tented area in search of blonde Harald. He discovered him eventually, gave him the list and told him to find the rest of the men. His final order was for all to report to him within an hour and left the man puzzled by his manner and sudden urgency.

Because many men had been sent to the centre of the city to keep order at the execution of Egbert, few were to be seen in the vicinity of the camp as

CHAPTER ELEVEN

Athyll slowly made his way to his quarters. It was a warm day and his leg was painful but he managed to disguise the limp so that it was not too evident.

He had almost reached the hut when he saw a woman, walking beside a pony, making her way toward the tented area. She had her back to him and he followed her. As he came up to her he called out, telling her to stop — it was a strict rule that women were not allowed in the encampment area unless they had authority to be there.

As she heard his voice she turned quickly. She recognised the voice now she was looking at the tall figure and was smiling.

'Ellen — it is you,' he said, surprised. She was the last person he had expected to see in this place. 'What are you doing here?'

She pointed to the two large sacks hanging on either side of the horse. 'I get the soldiers' clothes for washing and things that need to be mended,' she replied calmly enough but her heart was suddenly pounding. 'Athyll, sir, are you all right? You were not here to see that man tried.'

Her concern was plain. 'Yes, I should have been there,' he told her. After a pause he added: 'But I had other things to attend to.'

She caught the pony's bridle and looked up at him. 'Yes,' was all she could say in reply but as she began to move off again she offered up a silent prayer of thanks for his safe return from whatever adventure, dangerous as her instinct told her it must have been.

Now that Athyll was walking beside her all was suddenly changed. She had woken to a dull workaday world with nothing but a dreary prospect before her. Now it had been transformed into a magical existence she had never known at any time in her life.

She looked up at him, smiling. 'Athyll, will you walk with me to my work?' she asked, trembling a little at her boldness. He stopped in some surprise, about to tell her he could not, when she rushed on: 'Please, it is but a very short way.'

He looked down at the eager young face, framed with rich brown hair, and relented. At least, he told himself, he would be able to ask her about Medrin.

'As you wish,' he said, and took the pony's bridle from her. They walked together, past the sentry and out onto the rough cart track which led down to a farm. There was silence for some time — Ellen quite content to be beside Athyll and she could think of nothing to say.

'How was the girl Medrin at the trial of Egbert?' he said at last, in a matter-of-fact way.

'Oh, she was very well,' replied Ellen in the same tone of voice but pleased that he had spoken. Athyll waited to hear more from her but she fell silent again so he went on to say that he had been told the girl had been returned to her uncle.

'Yes, I think that was the best thing for her,' Ellen answered, then told the man about her work and how she disliked her master.

'But I have plans and will leave him as soon as I am able,' she ended eagerly. There was silence again as both became engrossed in their own thoughts and soon they were at the farm. The woman was inside the weaving hut and called out to Ellen. The girl was standing quietly beside the soldier now, wondering how to leave him, when the woman came rushing out. Then she saw Athyll and stopped short.

'Oh, who is this then?' she snapped.

''Tis a cavalryman from the soldiers' camp,' said Ellen proudly, then added: 'He has seen me safely back.'

The woman glared at her and ordered her back into the hut. But before she went Ellen turned to Athyll, took his hand and curtsied to him. The girl, with one last despairing look at the man, then went back to her work, quickly followed by the woman.

As he made to go back to the road Athyll could hear the scolding going on in the woman's harsh voice but his thoughts had turned again to other things. First to Medrin and wild fantasies about how he might get to meet her again, then, with an effort, he brought his mind back to more practical matters.

Chapter 12

It was all over. The crowd which had watched the execution had gone: the two hangmen recruited from local labourers had been in no hurry to remove the body of Egbert and had gone home for their morning meal. It hung grotesquely, swaying gently in the light breeze, the face swollen and blue, the eyes staring unseeingly in the final expression of fear.

Ellen, on her way to the encampment through the city, approached the place lightheartedly. Though she had heard the hanging was going to take place, she expected it to have been done with by the time she had arrived at the scaffolding. Now she was upon the scene and saw it in all its grim reality. She blanched, turned her face away and urged her pony into a trot from its measured ambling gait. A group of three youths approaching waved their rough caps and shouted obscenities at her. She ignored them and urged her horse to move faster. It stumbled, regained its balance quickly, then carried her towards the camp and out of their sight.

Still shaking slightly she set about her work and began to feel better. When she had finished she made her way slowly to the place where she had met Athyll. There was no sign of him and she became aware that the camp seemed strangely deserted. Despondently she went on her way until she saw a man supported by a crudely made crutch coming toward her. They met and he touched his forehead to her. As he made to move on she put her arm out and stopped him.

'I see you are wounded — has there been a battle?' she asked, fearing his answer. He studied her for a moment, wondering what her interest might be. He decided, watching her anxious expression, that she must be concerned about a particular man from the camp. She's a pretty young thing, he thought, and whoever it might be he is a lucky man.

'Was you looking for someone?' he asked, following his thoughts. A native caution told her not to give this stranger the truth but another more urgent demand for information about Athyll proved stronger.

She hesitated, then: 'Yes — there is a soldier who rides a fine black horse.' She paused again. 'I have some clothes for him here — I think his name is Athyll,' she added carefully, caution not deserting her entirely.

The man shook his head. 'They is more than one as rides that kind of horse, miss, but most of the soldiers is out — some guarding the King, some looking for the Danes. Your man could be with any of them lot,' he said, then moved on, leaving the girl none the wiser.

Athyll dismounted from Surgel slowly and painfully. He led the horse to a stream, its clear running water inviting both man and animal to drink. Athyll did so avidly, then found some shade under a tree and laid down, surrendering himself to the luxury of the first real rest for three days. His body, unusually succumbing to stress, ached and to this was added a more damaging state of despair. The recent short encounter with a small force of Welshmen, trying to take advantage of the present strain on the Saxons, had left him questioning his role in the scheme of things. And where the continued attempts of the enemy to crush the people of Wessex would end.

As he lay, the distant chatter of his men going unheeded, it was an embittered Athyll whose thoughts now centred on a vision of unceasing, cruel and demoralizing conflict. Many good people would die in the struggle, but for what purpose? To protect a good King, maybe, but would his forces be strong enough, as they had certainly not been for his predecessors?

He looked across at the figure of Surgel, contentedly grazing nearby, the sweat glistening on his sleek body. He needs a rub down, thought Athyll inconsequentially, then his vision became blurred and his eyes slowly closed. He found he and his men the centre of a force of a large group with the Danes hacking their way towards them. Suddenly they gave way and a figure on a big white horse emerged, making its way towards Athyll. As it got nearer he could see that it was Medrin, her hair flying in the wind, but instead of a sword she carried a scroll high in the air in her right hand. She pulled up sharply before Athyll and waved the paper in his face, taunting him.

'Here it is, proof that I am Queen of Wessex,' she cried exultantly. Then, laughing, she turned her horse and rode away through the massed ranks of cheering Danes. Athyll mounted and rushed forward to attack the nearest man but found his sword snatched out of his hand by something or someone and he fell off his horse. Oddly, this was not Surgel.

He awoke with a jerk as he felt a hand shaking him. 'Time we wus leaving, isn't it, sir?' a voice told him.

Athyll sat up and gathered his thoughts. He did not know how long he had slept but the sun had sunk to the horizon. He thought they might have been there for an hour or more.

The troop arrived back at Winchester some hours later. Athyll did not bother to report but went straight to his hut. He slept the clock round and was wakened by a man telling him that a girl wished to see him. It was Ellen. She apologised for disturbing him. In fact he welcomed the intrusion — it meant that he did not have to see anyone later.

'Are you ill?' she asked as she came to him as he lay on his bed.

He smiled at her concern. 'No, I am quite well,' he told her. The truth was that his head ached and the wound in his leg was throbbing.

'The war is lasting a long time,' she said.

'If there was but one it would not be so bad — there are several.' He paused and looked up at her. 'Does it worry you very much?'

'Yes,' was all she could reply. She could not put into words her fears for him and, though she had lost an older brother in a long-forgotten battle, she had only dim memories of him.

Athyll took a long drink of mead from a stone jar beside his bed. Ellen waited uncertainly, not wanting to leave and not knowing how to tell him that her work at the camp was to be ended. The man replaced the jar and saw that she was still with him. He wondered idly what it was she wanted. Clearly she had something to say but whatever it was he knew her well enough to realise that it would not be what might be going through the mind of a camp follower who came here from time to time.

'Why did you want to see me?' he asked, breaking the awkward silence.

His nearness and his invitation to confide in him brought sudden tears to her eyes but she forced them back so that he would not see them. He gestured for her to be seated on the nearby chair but she remained standing.

He waited and at last she spoke. 'I am not coming here any more. The old woman says that soldiers do not pay her for their washing.'

Athyll gestured impatiently. 'I am not surprised — they get little here beside their bed and food — not enough of that. We all know they often steal — if they do not pay it is because they have other uses for their money.'

'Yes, Athyll, but I will have no work or place to live,' Ellen told him earnestly. Though she was part of a tenant farmer's household there were only domestic duties for her and her lodging went with these.

The girl's look of despair and helplessness was one he had seen many times before on the faces of those who had suffered from loss of their homes or relatives. But where there would have been some feeling of compassion, now there was only one of numbness, of somehow being detached, an onlooker not involved in any way.

She watched him anxiously, not wanting to break his thoughts. He was about to say something non-committal to her when the door opened and one of the men who shared the hut entered. He was fully equipped with helmet and sword and as he stepped briskly into the small space he saw Ellen and stared hard at her. He turned to Athyll his expression showing his displeasure.

'I've been looking for you — I see I should have made my way here earlier.' He began unbuckling his sword and removed the rest of his equipment, throwing it on the bed beside Athyll. 'In case you have forgotten it is your tour of duty but Aldan wishes to see you before you start.' There was a brief pause as he looked at Ellen again. 'And get rid of her before you go.'

He turned and made to leave. Athyll was about to get up as though to follow him but changed his mind. Instead he called out after him: 'The girl works here — she wanted my advice.'

The man paused at the door, hesitated, then left without saying anything.

Athyll went to the girl and absently patted her shoulder. 'I'll see what can be done,' he told her but his mind was on other things. He saw Ellen to the door and after he had watched her go he collected his sword only, then slowly made his way to meet the Commander, not relishing the encounter. He was in no mood for any sort of questioning, his instinct telling him that this would be the reason for the meeting.

As he stepped inside Aldan's wooden structure, which was only marginally more permanent than the rest of the camp, the grizzled soldier, who looked older than his forty years, waved him to a wooden box which served as a seat. He stared hard at Athyll for a few moments, meanwhile the young man looked past him at a crudely drawn map on the wall behind, feigning lack of concern.

At last Aldan spoke. 'Athyll, you have been back for two days from your last patrol and I have had no report from you. Why?'

Athyll shrugged. 'There was nothing to report. We met a few Welshmen — there was nothing more than that.'

Aldan spat out an expletive, then went on: 'But you know the King wants all the information he can get, particularly at a time like this. Did you not think of taking a prisoner?'

'No, sir. I took them to be a hand of robbers roaming the country for any spoil they could get.'

There was a pause. 'How did you know they were Welsh? Can you be certain of that?'

'Yes, I am certain. We heard them calling to each other and we came upon a wounded man who said something foreign before he died.'

'And uniforms? Did they have any kind of military wear?'

'No, only swords.'

'As far as you could see?'

'Yes.'

Aldan stared hard at Athyll, closely studying his features. 'Very well, so be it. But I still need your full report.'

The words were rapped out sharply. Aldan was not a man to withhold his displeasure, despite his liking for Athyll and seeing the signs of battle weariness which he knew so well.

'You may have it now, sir,' replied Athyll dryly. The beginning of a smile came on the old soldier's face, then went as quickly as it had appeared. He turned back to the table and helped himself to some water straight from a jug.

There was a pause while Athyll recollected what had happened on his foray into the enemy-held land. Then he went on to give his account of how, when the small Saxon force reached an area near Gloucester, they had spotted a dozen or so horsemen following a rough path up to high ground. After deploying his men Athyll had caught the other group in a cross fire of arrows. Surprisingly, they had fled after one of them had fallen from his horse, shot through the chest. The rest of them were pursued for some distance but, when they approached a settlement of some four or five houses up in the hills, Athyll had decided not to follow them any further, believing that they were possibly part of a much larger force. 'That was all that happened, Aldan,' he concluded.

'Good — that was what I wanted.' He glanced up at the map. 'The area seems to confirm the existence of a Welsh group and most likely a large one, as you suspected.' Aldan continued to study the map, ignoring Athyll. It was his dismissal and Athyll left with relief, taking some pleasure from the thought that he had not come out of the meeting too badly.

Aldan remained deep in thought for a while, then made his way to the stables, collected his horse and rode into the city. He was soon with Sir Edwig, who had taken command of the local troops after the death of the Earl of Bedford. They talked for some time and, after Aldan had returned to the camp, Edwig sent for a messenger. The man was ordered to summon Galwain of Basing and two other Commanders to see Sir Edwig at his headquarters in the capital; the intention was to mount as large a force as possible and attack whatever enemy force was to be found in the north-western border area of Alfred's kingdom.

Whilst he was waiting for the commanders to arrive, Sir Edwig reported personally to the King and was given immediate approval for the operation. He also told Sir Edwig that, after several ships had been launched at London, he had moved the building of another fleet to Southampton and at this time was anxious for news of the progress of this development. The King now gave Edwig the responsibility of pursuing this information: the success of the new vessels had pleased him and he made it clear that superiority over the Danes at sea was as important as it was on the land.

Within twenty-four hours an army of men was moving out of Winchester in the direction of Gloucester and at the same time Athyll had been summoned once again into Aldan's presence. This time the meeting was short. 'Athyll, I have had word from Bowood that the King wants news of his ships — I am to send a man to Southampton for that purpose.' He paused, came to the front of the table to face Athyll. 'You are to go there without delay — your task will be to find the state of the fleet, what stage it has reached, what problems there might be that could delay progress. You have full authority to deal with anything that is in your power — what is important is that the work is moved forward as quickly as possible. The King needs those ships — and quickly!'

Aldan waited for questions. Athyll asked him about the number of ships and the type of men working on them.

'Something like thirty ships — the men are mainly local but there are some from Kent and some Frisians,' he was told. There was a moment's silence.

'Well?' asked Aldan impatiently.

'One more thing, sir. I feel that I would like some assistance. I need another man at least!'

Athyll was thinking that the task might be more complicated than it appeared at first sight and he had one soldier in mind who would not only be valuable for his reliability and common sense but also good company.

Aldan looked doubtful. He was not sure this was altogether right but on reflection he thought it might be a good thing. He had chosen Athyll for this expedition because he thought it would not be too onerous for him and in the hope that it would help restore him to the fitness that he would surely need in the coming months. At last he nodded his grudging assent, cautious not to commit himself too definitely.

Now, having received his instructions, Athyll went in search of Harald to tell him of the good turn of events and to beg, borrow or steal a horse for him. The man had always said he wanted to be a cavalryman, now he was to get his chance.

Chapter 13

The pony stood patiently while Ellen placed the two rough leather bags containing all her worldly goods across its back. They had been with her family for some years and had become worn but fortunately were able to hold what did not amount to much but was her own.

Ellen could hear the woman Agga sobbing in the hut nearby but ignored it. She was in a hurry to get away and she thought that the tears were not for her but because Agga would now be without any help at all. What the girl did not realise was that she would also miss Ellen's company, though she had never shown any need for it in the past. Ellen was about to get on to her mount when a voice called to her.

'Hold there, girl.' It was the farmer, John, and he came up to her, wiping his nose with the back of his hand as he did so. 'The horse — so ye're taking it, then? I wus thinking ye would sell it to us.'

'No, I told you — I need him.' Ellen stared coldly at the man then swung herself agilely up and settled herself on the pony.

'Ye'll never be able to keep it,' he shouted at her. 'No man will let his drudge have an animal with her.'

'Will they not? We shall see,' she called back, fervently hoping that the farmer would be proved wrong. Pointing at the hut she added: 'You had better see to your lady, she is in some distress,' then dug her knees into the horse's back and it moved off at a quick trot.

As she made her way to the encampment Ellen's emotions were mixed and a feeling of depression settled on her as it had done so frequently in the past weeks. She decided to see Athyll once again, as he had promised to help her but was afraid that he might not have been able to do anything in the short time that had passed since they had last met. So what could she do then? She put the thought impatiently from her mind and slowed the pony down to a walk; without consciously doing so she was now delaying the moment when she would know, for good or ill, what her future might be. Whichever it was, Ellen was one who usually had her feet on the ground and was harbouring no illusions.

She made her lonely way and when she eventually arrived at the camp it was silent and without any sign of life. Ellen's heart sank as she looked around her and saw the deserted pathways and empty open spaces. She knew this was a sign that a military operation had been started and the fewer the men at the camp the more important this would be. Her fear was that Athyll was with the troops and this was something she had not counted on as a possibility she would have to face at this time.

She decided to go straight to his hut and, after she had gone several hundred yards, she could see some activity in the distance ahead in the area where the horses were stabled. Encouraged by this, she carried on to the hut and dismounted, then sat on the ground while the pony pulled at the rough grass. She must have waited two hours before she heard voices. As they got nearer she could distinguish Athyll's faintly northern accent and another which she could not recognise.

The two men came into view and stopped short in front of the small body.

'Ellen, what in God's name are you doing here?' Athyll asked sharply. The girl got quickly to her feet and nervously tidied her hair. Harald smiled at her as a not unwelcome sight.

'I had nowhere else to go and you said you might help me,' she replied defensively. Athyll had to admit to himself that this was true but had forgotten about the girl's problems.

'Well, yes,' he said slowly, then added: 'I fear I have not been able to do anything for you — in fact I am on my way to Southampton in the morning. I am sorry but there is nothing I can do until I return.' He looked down at her then moved into the hut. But Ellen seized his arm, stopping him.

'Then take me with you — I will find something to do there,' she cried eagerly.

'No, I cannot do that,' he replied, shaking his arm free and entering the building quickly. Harald was not smiling, now that he was fully aware of the situation he followed Athyll, leaving Ellen outside by herself.

Athyll stood by his bed, inwardly cursing this difficulty which had arisen so near, and inconveniently, to his departure. Harald watched him, wanting

CHAPTER THIRTEEN

to defend the girl's intervention but wondering whether he had a right to say anything: he was taken with the girl and admired her spirit but thought that Athyll might misinterpret his motive in supporting her wish to accompany them on their way south.

At last courage overcame his discretion. 'Were ye not hard on the girl, sir?' he said tentatively, then, having ventured so far, went on: 'What harm would it do if she wus to come along?'

He waited for the reaction, fully expecting it to be a strong one. Had he but known it Athyll was wrestling with his conscience. He had certainly promised the girl he would help her, now she must think that she was the responsibility of the army, if not himself alone.

'What will come of her, sir?' ventured Harald once more.

Athyll turned to him, having made up his mind. 'Very well — she may join us to Southampton but there are conditions.' He paused and started to divest himself of his sword and top clothing. 'Her horse will be slow so I will go ahead and I should be able to make thirty miles or so by midday. You will have to follow on and meet me there.' He dropped on to his bed and pulled the cover round him. 'And remember, Harald, she is no whore,' he warned, finally.

Harald grinned and went out into the gathering dusk. He could just make out the small shape huddled on the ground, still waiting. 'It is all right, girl. He says that you can come with us.'

Ellen jumped up so quickly with pleasure at the news that she collided with the tall soldier. He took her by the shoulders and gently steadied her: looking down into that fresh young face, Ellen's eyes told him that he had done the right thing.

'He is a good man, that one,' he told her simply.

'Yes,' was all she could say. She turned to see to the pony, tethering it to a nearby post, then went with Harald into the hut. The other two occupants being away their bunks were free but the girl would have been pleased to sleep on the floor if need be. Two beds were on one side of the room, the second at right angles to the other, L-shaped. In the corner by the door was a small table and on the far side was the third bed, by itself. Harald guided Ellen to it, indicating that it was for her use, then left her.

Whilst he was undressing he could hear her moving about. He smiled, thinking she might be considering which clothes to divest. There was silence now so he got between the rough woollen bedding. He closed his eyes. Now he felt a hand on his arm and sat up.

'What is it — something amiss?' he whispered.

'Where is it?'

He stared at her. 'Where is what?'

She hesitated. 'The pot.'

The man was now completely mystified. 'What pot, girl?'

She sighed with exasperation. 'Why, the chamber pot, of course.'

Suddenly the light dawned on Harald and he laughed at the thought. The sound awoke Athyll. He sat up and saw the two figures at the bottom of his bed. He stared at them for a moment and was about to ask what was happening when Harald anticipated his question.

'She is asking for the pot, sir,' he said solemnly, trying to suppress his giggles. But he was unable to do so for long and laughed outright; he was joined by Athyll and both men were almost choking in their laughter. Ellen stood, her face reddening with embarrassment as she realised her mistake.

Athyll was the first to recover. He looked up at her. 'You had better do the best you can,' he told her. He lay back on the bed, covered himself and laughed again. But the humour of the situation was lost on the girl. When she had worked for the merchant Egbert there had always been something for use in the night and she saw no reason why one was not available in this case. With the laughter, subdued now, still ringing in her ears she went out into the night again, but thankful there was no-one about.

Next morning Athyll was up and on his way before the others stirred. Forgoing a meal, he decided to halt after he had covered a fair distance, then have something to eat and rest the horse. It was some thirty minutes after he had left the camp that Ellen and Harald were getting ready to follow. She had said nothing at all and now there was an awkward silence as they mounted their horses. As they moved off he was wondering whether he ought to apologise for the previous evening when she urged the pony into a trot.

Outside the camp she turned left but this was the wrong way. He called to her but she ignored him, then he called again. This time she realised that she might be going in the wrong direction and reined the horse to a sudden stop. She turned and saw Harald taking the opposite path. She caught up with him, the pony snorting with the sudden effort.

Harald gestured towards it with a gloved hand. 'The horse seems in trouble.'

'No, he is not — he is very well,' she put in quickly. Then added: 'I think he is only hungry,' fearing that she might still be put off from joining

Athyll. But she had no need to be worried on that count: Harald's concern was only for the animal.

As they went on slowly now, he asked: 'What is his name?'

'He does not have one,' she replied sharply, somewhat surprised by the question.

'Then we must give it to him,' he said, smiling down at her. 'What would you like to call it?'

She thought for a moment, trying to conjure something from her memory. She smiled as Athyll came to mind but knew that would not be acceptable. All the other male names that she could recall sounded silly for a horse — Edgar, Egbert, Oswald and so on, even Harald. She suddenly giggled, then told him: 'I can think of none.'

Harald had been doing his own reckoning. 'I think Wincher,' he said.

'Wincher?'

'Yes. He is from Winchester, so why not Wincher?'

She nodded, impressed by the simple reasoning and the word did not sound bad. He pulled his horse up and, as Ellen also stopped, he reached down and pulled his sword from its scabbard. Raising it over the pony's head in mock ceremony he intoned: 'Horse, I hereby dub thee Wincher and so honour the name all thy days.'

The girl laughed at the lighthearted fooling but it had the desired effect. As they started off again Ellen saw the man in a new light. Her first impression of him had been unpleasant and somehow she had resented the fact that he was going to accompany Athyll, not knowing that he had spoken to Athyll on her behalf. Now she was more cheerful than she had been when they started out that morning, more anxious than ever to carry on and meet Athyll at the end of their journey.

'Come on, show him what you can do,' she called to the pony and urged it into a trot. Harald soon caught up with her and together they proceeded in comfortable silence until he decided it was time to stop and rest. They came to an isolated farmhouse and bought food from an elderly sullen farmer, then found a verdant clearing in a wood nearby.

Dismounting, they saw to the horses, then sat together with their backs to a tree. As they ate she asked him about Southampton; he had to admit that he had never been there and only knew what Athyll had told him.

'It is to the south, a port on the stretch of water coming inland from the sea,' he added, remembering the map that Athyll had drawn in the dust with his finger but unable to think of the terms he had used.

Ellen was pleased with what she had been told. It meant that it was unlikely that there would be any suitable work for her in a place that was used mainly for shipbuilding. Since her purpose was to stay with Athyll this suited her very well.

It started to rain. The girl instinctively edged closer to the tree: her nearness disturbed the man and he stood hurriedly.

'I think we should be moving.' The statement was curt, thrown over his shoulder as he walked to the horses.

Ellen did not reply but went on eating. He mounted and came over leading the pony and threw the reins over to her.

Unaware of the reason for his suddenly leaving her side but not to be hurried, she carefully chewed each piece until the meagre food was finished.

Eventually they were on their way and neither spoke for the rest of the journey.

Arriving at the port in the driving rain, Athyll went straight to the nearest boatyard. To his intense irritation not a man was to be found working on a half-completed ship and one that was apparently in the process of being started, only long planks of wood being evident, stacked beside the frame which would take them when the construction work began. There was no cover on either of the frames and Athyll looked around for a place where the men might be sheltering.

Away to the south he saw the rain dancing on the waters of the estuary; to the east and west there was nothing but bleak open spaces. But following the course of the water behind him, going beyond the stretch of sand left by the receding tide, he could see a building settled at the bottom of the cliff. It was long, with a strong wooden roof and Athyll purposefully made his way toward it.

It was further away than it appeared and took him several minutes to reach it. As he approached he could hear several voices. Lifting the latch of the door he did not stand on ceremony and kicked it open. He was met by a damp, smelly atmosphere and the surprised stare of ten men sitting round a rough table. One of them rose and came towards Athyll menacingly. Then he saw the tall figure with his military equipment and stopped short.

'What is this — who are ye?' he asked nervously, fearing that a possible Viking raid they had been warned about was actually happening.

CHAPTER THIRTEEN

Athyll looked round, taking in each man in turn. They were a mixed group: some foreign-looking with their shorter hair and better clothing, the rest probably local men. But they were all tall and muscular.

'Why are you not working on those ships?' he asked them.

'We are waiting for wood.' It was the first man who spoke. He was tall and thin, with long straggling hair and a scar on his left cheek from ear to chin.

'There is some out there,' replied Athyll, curtly.

''Tis not enough — we need small pieces.' He glanced warily at the soldier. 'What is your business here, sir?' he added cautiously, still not sure with whom he was dealing. Two more men stood and the three of them faced Athyll. He put his hand on his sword in an automatic gesture; none of them were armed, so he replaced it by his side but remained watchful.

'I come from the King — he wants news of the state of his fleet and I am to give it to him.' He looked round for the reaction. Apart from the small section of the aliens, who were staring at him, not understanding, the rest seemed to have accepted his statement, if not willingly. He went on: 'Now, tell me where I can find the shipbuilder, Elfrick?'

They did not know — the man moved about the yards and from place to place, he was told.

It was clear that this meant a search but Athyll had anticipated it as the first task. Now, having made his point he left the men, hoping that it would have made some useful impression on them.

Remounting the horse he reminded himself that Harald and the girl should have arrived by this time. His thoughts lingered ill-humouredly for a moment on Ellen's unwelcome intrusion then he continued on his way. The rain had now eased to a fine drizzle and the other yards being close by he was soon making an inspection of them.

The first was more promising than that previously seen: two ships almost completed and the men were Saxon, all working. The second, again, had one completed awaiting launch into the water but nothing else to show. But he counted four ships already riding the tide on both sides of the estuary. Approaching three men gathered round a mast about twelve feet tall, he want to one who was arranging the placing of the timber.

'Where can I find Elfrick?' he called. They appeared not to have heard because the wind shipped the words away but now he was beside the group. He asked again, almost into the man's ear. He turned, saw the tall figure and grinned at Athyll.

'Elfrick? Did ye say Elfrick?'

'Yes — where can I get him?'

The man, about forty years of age, with a large beard but very bald, nodded to the others and took the soldier's arm.

'I know where he is — getting supplies — but who are ye?'

This at last confirmed some part of what those at the first yard had told him, thought Athyll, and he explained his mission to this man who seemed to be alert and reliable.

'And I am Wilfred, a sailor of this town. Come with me.' The man stepped on to the path and walked quickly from the yard, Athyll close behind but having some difficulty in keeping up.

As they went past the yards and out on to the cart track, which was the way into the town, Athyll was beside his companion.

'This mission of yours is sore needed,' Wilfred told him, slowing his pace.

'Yes?' said Athyll shortly. Although he had formed a quick impression of the position he waited for the man to elaborate. Wilfred was silent. 'Well, what are the problems?'

'Best let Elfrick tell you that,' was the grim answer.

'What is he like, this man?' asked Athyll. He was beginning to have doubts about the real extent of his involvement in this, his first attempt as a royal envoy.

Wilfred's grin was without mirth. 'He knows about ships but little about men,' he replied. Though curtly put, it told Athyll what he wanted to know.

They soon reached the outskirts of the town, with a few modest homesteads dotted here and there off the rough track. After they had passed them and came in sight of more buildings in the near distance, Athyll stopped.

'Wait — I have to meet another man who has come from Winchester. I must see him first.'

''Tis not a big place — you will find him.'

'Not a monastery?' asked Athyll. These often gave shelter, even food, to travellers but would not take a female.

'Bless you, no. Elfrick hates the clergy — there is a house set up by a man and his lady to look after such as him and your fellow.'

Later they stood outside the building. It had been built by the man himself with the help of the local mason and was indeed one of the most solid structures in the town. And here he found Harald with Ellen, recently

CHAPTER THIRTEEN

arrived, in an argument with the woman. ''An' I tell ye — this is not a bawdy house,' she shouted at them.

'And I am not a whore,' Ellen yelled back.

Athyll stepped between the two and pushed them apart. The woman stared at him in surprise and Ellen backed away when she saw the look on his face. Athyll gestured to Harald standing neutrally in the background. He had been quietly enjoying the row between the girl and her older opponent, now he realised that it might not prove to be so amusing after all.

'Harald, come with me.' He turned to Wilfred. 'Would you take us to Elfrick, then try to settle whatever ails this woman?'

Wilfred nodded, then took them up the short staircase and knocked on the door of a room at the end of a narrow passageway. Without waiting for a reply Wilfred opened the door and they entered. Seated at a table was a small, plump man with brown hair, carefully groomed, falling to his shoulders. He sat, in elegant contrast to his wet, dishevelled visitors, and eyed them with some disdain.

'They is two men from Winchester,' Wilfred told him then added, with relish: 'From the King.' Then, grinning, he left them. Elfrick's attitude had now changed completely. He jumped up and extended his hand. He asked them to be seated but as the only place available was a small bed Athyll declined the offer. Elfrick returned to his chair and watched the two soldiers nervously.

'This is an honour, sirs, but could I ask the purpose of your visit to Southampton?'

'Very simply, to find the state of the King's ships,' replied Athyll. 'I have been to two of the yards and I am not satisfied with what I have seen.' He paused, not impressed with the man.

Elfrick spread his hands in depreciation. 'There have been problems — there is a shortage of pine and I find the Friesians do not understand exactly what has to be done.'

Though this tallied with what Athyll had already learnt, he wanted to know more. 'Yes, but how serious are these difficulties and what is being done to deal with them?'

'All that is possible,' replied Elfrick stiffly. 'I am well aware of the need of these ships to the King and have used all means to build them.' He paused to take a drink and stared resentfully at Harald as though he had seen him for the first time. Then went on: 'I am waiting to see two men about a supply

115

of wood — they have possibly been delayed by the storm but I am expecting them to arrive at any time.'

Athyll ignored what he thought to be an exaggerated reference to the weather. 'Does the wood have to be pine?'

'That is what I need to know. Generally only that is used because its tar content helps to make it waterproof but oak is also a likely source but more costly,' said Elfrick, responding eagerly to a question which he believed to have some relevance.

Athyll nodded. 'I would like to join you when these men arrive,' he said.

Leaving a disconsolate shipbuilder they found Wilfred at a table by himself tucking into a dish of mutton stew. Harald eyed the food enviously.

'Can we eat, Athyll?' he asked hopefully.

'Yes, see what you can get from the woman.' Seated at the table he stretched himself wearily and closed his eyes. Wilfred went on eating. 'I had to take the lass to a friend,' he said at last, without looking up.

'What?' sighed Athyll.

'They would not have the girl here — I had to leave her with a friend,' the man repeated.

'Good — so that is settled,' Athyll said, suddenly realising and dismissing the matter as Harald approached with the thin, harassed woman and welcome plates of hot food. While they ate Wilfred regaled the soldiers with tales of visits to Frisia and Gaul, where he had seen the buying of English boys on the orders of the Pope, so that they could serve in monasteries and be trained as priests. When the two men expressed their surprise that this should happen he explained that the boys had been captured and would have otherwise been sold into slavery.

He proved to be an entertaining talker, with Athyll and Harald mainly the listeners. But this recollection of foreign places brought Medrin to mind for Athyll; he saw her tall figure and proud bearing and the expression which, though haughty, hid a restless spirit. At this point he suddenly announced that he was going to see Elfrick again and make arrangements for the next day as the arrival of his two callers now seemed likely.

'You had better come too,' he told Wilfred.

And so it was that the three of them would meet early in the morning and go to the yards regardless of whether the timber advisers had arrived or not. Returning to the large room downstairs with Wilfred for a last drink, Athyll was surprised to find the place deserted except for one small figure standing forlornly by a table.

CHAPTER THIRTEEN

'Ellen, why have you come back here?'

'I had to see you,' she said, casting a nervous glance first at Athyll and then at Wilfred.

'But I was told you were settled.' Athyll seated himself and called loudly for the woman Rona.

Wilfred placed his hand on Athyll's shoulder.

'I will not stop for the drink — think I had best be going,' he said, understanding.

Ellen stood uncertainly, the man staring hard, waiting. Then the woman appeared with a small jug of mead. She saw Ellen and was about to say something when Athyll put out his hand to stop her. Taking the jug he told her: 'It is all right, woman — she has business with me.'

Rona gave him a look full of meaning, then left with an ill-tempered glance at the girl.

Athyll sipped his drink without taking his eyes off Ellen.

'It is Wincher,' she said at last.

Athyll nearly choked on a generous mouthful. 'Wincher,' he gasped. 'Who the hell is he?'

'It is my horse — Wincher is the name Harald gave to him.'

Athyll put his mug on the table and sighed. The day was beginning to catch up with him. 'So — what is the matter with Wincher?' he asked wearily.

'He is sick of something — he will not eat and he has a cough.' She paused and took a step nearer to him. 'You know about horses, Athyll, and I thought you could help him.' It was the first time she had called him by name but it seemed to have come to her naturally. He did not seem to have noticed and got up slowly to his feet. He had just remembered that Surgel had had very little food that day. He went to the door and gestured for Ellen to follow.

They went first to Surgel, then some half-mile to a small shed beside a cottage building. Athyll listened to the cough, looked into the pony's mouth, then felt his neck and stomach.

'There is some sickness but I think it is not serious. Don't feed him for a day and keep him warm all the time.'

'Yes, of course.' She took the thick shawl from her shoulders. 'I will not need this. I am very warm in the cottage with two kind people.' She moved forward and placed the shawl over the pony's back. They were very close

117

now. She looked up at him and slowly took his hand. 'I love you, Athyll,' she said simply.

He looked into the warm brown eyes and felt the soft body move closer to him. He hesitated, but only for a moment. She threw her arms round him, then their lips met.

Later they made a bed for the horse from the straw still warm from their bodies. As they made to part she gave him an artless smile. He looked at her flushed, eager face, then put his arm gently round her; it was more like the action of an affectionate friend than lover.

All next day was spent in the yards with Athyll inspecting, questioning, criticising, cajoling the people involved. As a result of all this, he found that apart from the shortage of wood there was dissatisfaction among the men employed on the ships. Differences of outlook, of loyalties, had led to disputes, even fighting among some of the most desperate group of men with whom Athyll had ever had to deal. But when the soldiers had given assurances from the King, there were signs of improvement and Elfrick became more confident and cheerful, adding some useful advice and assistance.

After the long and tiring work had been done, Wilfred took Athyll and Harald to his friend's house where a good meal had been prepared and was waiting for them. There was home-baked bread, large helpings of fresh fish, apple dumplings, all washed down with strong local ale. Ellen had helped to prepare the food and her eyes shone with pleasure as the men ate with relish.

There was little talk but when they had finished Athyll thanked the woman. 'That is the best meal I have had for many a day,' he told her, his companions finding no disagreement.

Afterwards they all went back to the house where an entertainment — which included a ballad singer and a girl contortionist — was going on. As they entered Athyll protectively took Ellen's hand and led her to the other side of the room. There were no seats so they had to stand until one young man, full of drink, fell off a long wooden form to the floor. His friends were about to help him up when Athyll placed the girl in the empty space. Another noisy youth was about to grasp her when he saw the soldier and changed his mind.

While Ellen watched the contortionist entranced, the three men went in search of ale which seemed to flow freely. And so the thing dragged on until the performers, growing tired of doing the same thing again and again, finally went. The place gradually emptied of customers who were getting rowdier and rowdier. Eventually, when the landlord had thrown the last of them out, the place returned to some semblance of normality. In spite of having had his fill of mead and ale, Athyll insisted on escorting Ellen back to the cottage but Harald, seeing his state, accompanied them.

Much to the younger man's surprise, Athyll was up early the next morning and showing no signs of being affected by his drinking of the previous night. They went to the yards for more inspection; about midday Elfrick's men eventually turned up. Athyll was able to get more information from them and a final tally of the situation. Now it was clear that the ships could be built more quickly; oak would be a suitable wood, with a tar base, and with the Frisians eventually separated from the Anglo-Saxons there should be an end to their misunderstandings and rivalry.

Having satisfied himself that he had done all he could and anxious to get away, Athyll decided to return immediately to Winchester. He was on the road with Harald when they met Ellen coming towards them leading the pony.

'I thought she wus going to find work here,' said Harald meaningly. He suspected that the relationship between the two had changed and was resentful, thinking of the warning this man had given him the day before they had set out.

'I am going to find a place for her with Lady Bedford,' replied Athyll, spurring his horse and riding on, leaving the others to follow.

Chapter 14

After Medrin had been escorted from Winchester to Guthrum's headquarters in East Anglia, her meeting with her Uncle was brief. He greeted her affectionately but seemed preoccupied and, after telling her that his decision to let her join his army in England had been a mistake, he told her of his future plans. She was to go first to his hunting lodge at Hollingstedt and stay there until he could join her, then they would both go to Haedum, the busy port on the Jutland peninsula which was a clearing house for the North sea trade and military movement. It was here he held court and planned his operations against the English.

The short meeting was over. Guthrum called his servants and ordered Medrin to go with them. For her, being united again with her uncle — her only family — had been a great disappointment. She had not known for certain what it might bring for her but she had not expected such drastic and rapid developments. At the least she had expected a few days with him in East Anglia and a chance to talk to him. Surprisingly, he had shown no interest at all in her experiences with the Anglo-Saxons and this had distressed her. So, numb with emotional pain that somehow she managed to conceal, she said little. At her dismissal she dazedly remounted her horse, escorted on both sides by two soldiers with a serving woman in the rear. Upset and irritable, she shouted at one of the men when he came too close to her as they made their way out of the encampment.

After two hours' journey they arrived at a small bay where a large ship was riding the waves at anchor. The Danes had virtual control of the whole of the East Anglian coast so they were able to land and leave at will. One of the soldiers called to a man standing in the prow, 'Are you the ship for the homeland?'

'Yes — we have been waiting a long time. Come on, you will have to hurry or we shall lose the tide.'

Now Medrin panicked. She did not want to leave on this ship and sought frantically for an excuse, any ruse to stay behind. She had noticed a small building at the top of the rise from the beach, possibly a fisherman's hut. She suddenly decided that the fainting fit was the simplest and best way out for her. At least it would delay going on board and give her time to think of a more permanent solution. So she swayed in the saddle and, taking some risk, she slid off the horse to the ground. The nearest man quickly dismounted and went to her. She was breathing hard and with her hidden hand she was pinching the back of her leg to make herself blanch. The woman had now joined the man and eyed the girl for a few moments.

'It is nothing bad. She will be well enough in a day or so — just take her to the boat.' She looked at Medrin suspiciously, prepared to believe that she was ill but that it would only be temporary. Her orders had been strict; to stay with the girl until she had reached the hunting lodge.

The soldier seemed uncertain what to do and the woman repeated her instruction. He hesitated, then with a quick movement he picked up Medrin in strong arms with ease. She slowly opened her eyes and began to scream from the humiliation of her position and the frustration of her plan. The man ignored her cries and purposefully carried on to wade into the water towards the ship. There was a crew of six on board and they watched with amusement, one of them calling out obscenities. The woman servant, hurrying along behind, became angry and shouted at him to be quiet but he pretended not to hear. As they reached the vessel Medrin was handed over the gunwale to the man in the prow, still struggling and screaming. As he placed her firmly on the deck she swore and went to hit him but he dodged back quickly, leaving her sobbing. The soldiers now went back to their horses and, taking the riderless ones in tow, they moved off, both thankful to be rid of a task they considered undignified for warriors.

Borka, the serving woman, was helped on board with some difficulty because of her weight and there was more vulgar comment from the crewman. She went to him and brought a plump hand to his face with some force.

'Now, no more of that talk or you will be in trouble,' she shouted, making sure the other men could hear her. He stared at the woman blankly, but said

122

nothing so she hit him again. 'Do you understand me, you oaf?' she yelled. The sailor was about to say something, glanced furtively at Medrin and the servant, then changed his mind and simply nodded. Borka went to Medrin, who was sitting on the deck. The sobbing had ceased but she was staring at the land she was about to leave, miserably conscious of all it had come to mean to her and bitterly regretting the mistake of going back to Guthrum. It was from a feeling of loyalty that she had returned to him and she felt free to make her own choices as she had always done as a member of the Viking nobility. Clearly this was not to be the case from now on and the thought made her numb with despair.

Borka was seriously concerned about her charge and turned to the man who appeared to be in control of the ship. 'The lady is of noble blood and is ill — she needs rest and quiet.'

He could see that Medrin was far from well and took the rest on trust. There was a crude, tent-like structure on the deck. He gestured to it with a muscular arm. 'That is all we have.' He turned and ordered the other men to hoist the sail. It did not take long and as they tacked into the wind the light vessel began to move slowly out of the bay.

Borka helped the distressed girl to her feet and went to the opening of the flimsy shelter. She peered inside and grunted irritably when she saw a pile of dirty rope and stone bottles for what might have been water or liquor. She called out to the men and one came after the sail had been safely secured.

'The place is dirty and there is no room,' she complained.

The skipper came to the women. Taking off his leather jacket he put it around Medrin's shoulders. 'Take out the bottles and leave the rest,' he told his crewman. To Medrin he added: 'I'm sorry,' and went back to the mast where the sail was taking the wind well and the ship was gathering speed.

The place was cleared and Medrin crawled in. Once there she had no choice but to sit with her back to the rope and with her knees under her chin, too tired to notice the discomfort. The woman Borka looked in, was satisfied, and squatted her plump form outside, prepared now to get some sleep.

It was a smooth crossing but Medrin, normally a good sailor, was sick and had to endure the stench of the vomit for the rest of the voyage. And after nearly two days, which seemed an eternity to her, the ship sailed into a small, crowded harbour at Haedum. Feeling very weak she was helped ashore by Borka and one of the crew and was taken to a rough wooden building on the edge of the town. Offered a meal, she refused and asked for a bath and a change of clothing. There were only women in the place but they seemed surprised at her preference. Medrin irritably insisted and at last they obeyed with bad grace because the bath meant extra work, whilst the food was already prepared. She had lost a lot of weight in the last few days and they were even more appalled when they saw her thin body, which was considered a sign of weakness and infertility in Nordic women. As she stepped into the tub of lukewarm water which had been hastily prepared one of the women muttered, 'She should be eating, not wasting good water.'

After the quick bath Medrin still refused to eat. Instead she now demanded to be left alone so that she could rest. Again this caused resentment among the women; they had been told the girl would not be staying but go on to the lodge after a short stop on landing from the ship. But, backed by Borka, she got her way and was taken reluctantly to a room where there was a bed. It was bare and ricketty but Medrin slept almost as soon as she laid her head down.

It was almost eighteen hours later when she awoke. Her head throbbed but generally she felt better and was ready to leave; within a short time Medrin and the servant Borka had collected everything they needed, including horses, and were on their way north to the lodge which was going to be her home until the man who was virtually her lord and master decided otherwise.

Hollingstedt was nothing but a small village of a few huts and a large building used rarely these days by Guthrum and his close associates. It was set back in a small wood a mile from the sea so it provided hunting on land and water. Here there were twenty hours of darkness during the winter and it was almost inaccessible then because of heavy snowfalls. When the two women arrived they aroused great curiosity among the few inhabitants — some dozen women and children and one old man. They rarely had visitors and when these did come they were always men. All stared now as the two clopped by; the children seemed to be more interested in the horses, one brave boy went up to Medrin's and stroked its side. It reared and the boy was pulled sharply away but she steadied it and pushed through the small crowd.

At the lodge she was given a room of her own but there were several women in attendance. In the days which followed they kept close at hand; at first Medrin took little notice of this but after a while it began to irritate her.

CHAPTER FOURTEEN

Rested and with her strength coming back she found that when she wanted to explore the countryside on foot she would always be accompanied; going on horseback was forbidden.

Though her activities were strictly limited, what she was able to rule out for herself were lessons in weaving. In spite of repeated attempts to involve her she steadfastly resisted them. And she found that her favourite exercise of walking caused some discomfort among the companions not very well fitted for trudging in country mostly wooded and uneven. As her spirit and strength improved, Medrin played with them by going on ahead as fast as she could, leaving the others to follow out of breath and silently cursing her. Eventually they formed a rota system, which meant that each of them had days of rest in between their day of duty.

To relieve the monotony of her existence and her boredom, the girl devised games for the children to play and she became very popular with them. Being in a similar situation she was able to identify her life with theirs and her time spent in their company was the most enjoyable.

She was playing a game of hide-and-seek with the very young children when Grunwalde arrived. The woman watched for a moment, then called out sharply: 'Are you Medrin?'

Medrin looked up as the harsh voice rapped out and saw a tall thin woman, sharp-featured and pock-marked, looking down at her. From her vantage point on a big horse she appeared an awesome figure but Medrin answered calmly, 'Yes.'

'Then come with me, my lady.' The tone was more polite now but firm. As Grunwalde moved off and turned her back on the small group it was clear that Medrin was not expected to argue.

'I am sorry, children,' Medrin told them, then followed the horse. 'Who are you and what do you want with me?' she shouted. One of the children began to cry. Medrin hesitated, then went back to her and took her hand. 'I will be back soon,' she promised. Grunwalde had almost reached the lodge and spurred the horse; arriving at the door she dismounted with a quick athletic movement and stood at the door waiting.

Medrin came to her and was about to ask her again what her business was when the woman stood aside and gestured for her to enter. 'Please.' The icily polite voice grated on the girl. Medrin paused, then stamped inside, bumping into a woman who was about to come out. The girl mumbled an apology and Grunwalde asked for a quiet room. Once there, she asked for a cold drink and asked Medrin to sit. She remained standing.

'Now, you wanted to know about me. I am Grunwalde and my work here will be to take charge of this place until the men arrive.'

'Who sent you?' asked Medrin, going straight to the point.

'I was about to tell you.' The dark eyes stared hard at her, then she went on: 'I should have been here before but was delayed.' Grunwalde paused again and was about to speak when the door opened and her drink was brought to her. She sat now and sipped it without looking at Medrin.

Then: 'You were going to tell me who sent you,' Medrin reminded her coldly.

Grunwalde finished her drink and stood again. 'It was Othene.'

There was another pause and Medrin was becoming irritated by what she thought was an attempt to provoke her; the woman was playing a game with her but one which had a sinister undertone. 'And who is he?' The frigid tone was still showing Medrin's displeasure.

A thin smile appeared on the sharp features. 'He, as you put it, is the commander of the garrison at Haedum.' She sat now and added: 'He is the most powerful man here.'

Medrin's heart missed a beat. This was more news to trouble her. 'But I am in the care of my uncle Guthrum,' she protested.

'Until Lord Guthrum returns you are the subject of Othene.' The woman stood and gathered her gown, dismissing the matter. 'Now I must see the other women.'

So, having spoke to all those at the lodge, making her presence felt in no uncertain way, Grunwalde took the best room for herself — which happened to be Medrin's — and retired with orders to be called within an hour, the period of time she boasted was all she needed to be refreshed.

Chapter 15

The early morning sun filtered through the tall trees, the heavy foliage of summer casting shadows on the earth. This was the only time of day Medrin felt free and able to indulge herself with hopeful thoughts. She would retire as early as cleaning, cutting wood and other tasks would allow, then she would be up soon after dawn and go out into the woods. After sitting deep in reflection for some time she gathered wild herbs — her excuse if Grunwalde wanted to know where she had been — and returned to the house.

The woman Helge was lighting wood under a big pot in the large outhouse which served as a kitchen. Borka had long since been sent back to Haedum and Helge was the only person Medrin trusted at the lodge. Her face, red from the effort and warmth, looked up at the girl and smiled.

'You are up early again.'

'Yes.' Medrin handed her the herbs. 'Is there anything I can do?'

'You can mix dough for the bread — it is all ready on the table.' The fire was going now. She stood and straightened her back. 'There — I think I will go and take this underskirt off, it is so warm.'

She turned to the open door but Medrin stopped her. 'Helge, when are the men coming?'

The woman looked surprised. 'I think it is the end of the month. Why?'

'Oh, I am expecting my uncle to be with them, that is all.'

Helge appeared to be embarrassed now. This was not the sort of question she liked to be asked; there was only one person who gave out any information at the lodge. She nodded, smiled nervously and hurried out.

Suddenly the clear morning air was filled with cries of pain. They came across the courtyard from the house and Medrin rushed out to catch up with Helge, who had broken into a shambling run.

Inside, at the bottom of the short staircase, they met Edda, one of the four women who shared the room and the work at the lodge.

'Brod — it is Brod,' she gasped. Medrin pushed her and got to the top of the stairs as Grunwalde came out of the narrow passage. She held a thick leather strap in her hand. The screams from the room behind had given way to choking sobs. Medrin took a step forward, about to protest, then saw the look on the woman's face. Red blotches etched in the lines on cheeks and neck; the veins stood out on the temples and ice-blue eyes stared hard at Medrin. Now, as she stood there uncertainly, the door opened slowly. Brod was seen standing there, naked, with great weals on her thick flesh. She looked up, reddened eyes deep-set in her coarse features, greying hair matted with sweat. She tried to speak but no words came as she fell, losing consciousness.

Medrin turned quickly and ran back down the stairs and across the yard to the outhouse. She took a drink of water and sat heavily on an upturned barrel, the nearest thing. As she slowly collected her thoughts Edda and Helge came in. Edda was saying something but Medrin was not listening. She had come to a decision.

The morning's work went on without any sign of Brod or Grunwalde. Then she appeared at the house in the late afternoon whilst a meal was being taken quickly by the others. Her orders, as usual, were short and sharp. She waited for some show of understanding, only Edda smiled and nodded. Then she added, 'Brod was a thief and a liar,' and left. But the message was plain.

That night Medrin found an excuse to stay behind after Edda and Helge had gone to their beds. She managed to get a few essential things together and, when she thought all was quiet, she went quietly to the stables situated fifty yards from the main building. She went to the horse that had brought her there, a chestnut roan. It raised its head and snorted; Medrin had to quieten it with a piece of bread she had thought to bring. She looked for a saddle and bridle but could not see them. Not wasting any more time she climbed on to the horse's bare back and urged it forward out of the open door. It was a dark night and she made her way cautiously past the outhouse into the courtyard. She was level with the lodge and, breathing a soft sigh of relief, was about to break out into a trot when a dark figure sprang out in

128

front of her. The horse reared, then came to a halt. Looking up at her was the unmistakable face of Grunwalde.

'I have been waiting for you, Medrin. Edda came to me and told me that you were not in your room at this late hour.' The voice, though soft, was more menacing than ever.

After weeks of treatment which had sought to humiliate her in every possible way, Medrin was not to be daunted now she had the chance to escape. 'Get out of my way, woman, or I shall run you down,' she said calmly, but with meaning.

Grunwalde made no move so the girl edged the horse forward slowly. There was still no movement from the dark shape so Medrin slapped the roan's rear smartly and it suddenly sprang forward. There was a cry of fear and the figure disappeared. Medrin felt a sharp thud as the horse's hoof hit something but now that her way was clear she forced it into a gallop and sped on into the night. Once clear of the lodge, and the horse having found the track, she slowed down, leaving it to guide her through the darkness.

The rough road led along the coast and Medrin could hear the sound of the waves on the rocks below. She stopped for a moment, listening with pleasure and drew in a deep breath of the keen salt air. Now there was a new sound, the quick clop of hooves coming from behind her. She turned but could see nothing; straining to listen again the sound persisted. Then the sight of a horse came in view with a dark shape astride it.

Fearfully Medrin watched as it came closer and closer until it reached her. A thin but strong arm reached out and caught her hand, the face was pushed so close to Medrin that she pulled back in horror. It was white, like a ghost, but on one side there was a terrible gash that reached from above the eye down to the corner of the mouth. The blood was still oozing from it and emphasised the paleness of the rest of her face.

Medrin felt a sudden tug at her arm and almost fell from her horse. Snatching it quickly away she regained her balance but this time a hand caught in her hair. She tried to turn the horse and it moved part of the way, the grip on the hair tightened. Releasing a hand from the reins she swung her arm round with all the force she could muster. She felt the impact on the other's body, there was a muffled cry and her hair became free. As she made to move off her leg was grasped and she was pulled down before she realised what had happened.

Medrin came off the horse so suddenly and heavily that she fell on top of the woman. They were so close their faced nearly touched; blood was staining Medrin's dress. With a quick roll to one side she was able to stand again and tried to grasp the horse's mane. As she did so two hands seized her neck and started to squeeze. As Medrin's vision began to blur she reached up and tried to pull the grip away from her neck, at the same time she kicked out behind her. The grip slackened, then she got it away altogether, twisted round and faced Grunwalde.

The woman hesitated, wiped the blood away from her eye and lunged forward. Medrin jumped to one side and Grunwalde, taken by her own momentum, fell into the rough undergrowth on the edge of the track. She got up but her foot slipped on the loose soil and she fell back and down some way onto the side of the cliff. Medrin ran to the edge and looked down. She could see nothing but heard the faint cry: 'Help me, please help me.' Stretching her hand down there was no responding touch.

Still calm, the girl got up and went to Grunwalde's horse. Releasing the bridle and reins she ran back to the spot where the cries were still faintly to be heard. The reins were long and Medrin felt a tug and started to pull. There was no movement at first.

'Put your feet on the face of the cliff and try to climb,' she shouted. Waiting a moment, she started to pull on the reins once more. Then she sensed the weight at the other end beginning to move. She stepped back and continued to pull, then suddenly there was no weight at all. A long bloodcurdling cry sent an echo on the still night, and Medrin was left staring at the bridle with the broken reins hanging from it. She walked unsteadily to the grass verge which masked off the cliff face and looked down but there was only darkness.

Medrin awoke to find herself in a wooden structure that could have been anything from a grain storehouse to a small animal shelter. She had been lying on bare boards with her arm as a pillow. She felt stiff and her whole body ached. Sitting up she saw the bloodstains on her dress and the horror of the previous night came back to her. Even with no feeling of guilt the sight of that stricken face would stay with her for ever.

She went to the door and looked out. There was no one about but she decided not to risk an encounter during the day, so avoiding awkward questions. She went back and lay down again, sleeping and waking in turns until darkness came. There was no hunger now, only an intense tiredness and numbness of feeling.

Outside the hut she found that the horses were gone, though she felt sure she had left them there. It had occurred to her that she might have been able to sell them but was not too concerned about their loss. Her immediate problem was what to do next. She was determined to get back to England and Athyll one way or another. But having got this far the most difficult part still had to be overcome. Borka. The name suddenly came to her. She was here in Haedum, a port constantly used for transport across the North Sea. And she knew who Medrin was, a further advantage in any attempt to get a passage.

Medrin quickly ripped the bottom of her dress and, putting the remnant round her head and shoulders, she made her way out. The night was still and she was thankful for the warmth since she was wearing little clothing apart from a thin underskirt and dress, and she had no footwear. Finding a rough track she followed it and soon the shape of buildings came into sight.

In these close-knit ports with their interlocking occupations most people knew what others were doing and where they might be found. What Medrin wanted was to ask until she found someone who could take her to Borka, or to someone who did know her. A mist was coming in from the sea, but she was now clearly among the buildings and the vague shapes of the people moving about could be seen. She stopped the first as it came close to her. He was an elderly man with a long white beard. She hesitated but, when he stood beside her, said, 'I am looking for the woman Borka — do you know her?'

He stared and she repeated the question. He shook his head and shuffled on.

The next person, a woman, directed her to an eating house on the quayside. But when she got there she found that the person she had been sent to was known as Borge. She proved to be a large cheerful woman, who helpfully recognised the mistake and took trouble to get more information from Medrin about the woman she was looking for.

'Ah, a serving woman, you say.' She thought for a moment. 'Only two people in this town has them — Meron the harbour master and . . .' her voice dropped to a respectful whisper, 'the Lord Othene.' Of the two, Medrin was sure that Borka would be with the military.

'Where can I find his servants?' she asked quickly.

The woman returned to her chore of gutting fish. 'His household is up on the hill, outside the town.'

When this vague direction was given more substance, Medrin thanked her and made her way along the street. The mist was lifting slightly and there were more people about. Climbing to the top of the steep hill she came at last to a large, rectangular-shaped building raised on stilts from the ground with a set of wooden steps leading up to a double front door. In a semicircle some distance away there were a few small huts. This had to be the place but there was no way of knowing where Borka might be. She suspected it would be in one of the huts but she could hardly walk up to the door and ask. Fortunately she could hear voices coming from somewhere; there was no-one in sight so she ran to the back of the small buildings. There was nothing she could do now except wait — in hope.

She settled herself beside a tree in a nearby copse on the edge of the encampment but kept the main building and huts in view as much as possible. She felt tired and hungry and after a while found herself nodding in the heat. The noisy activity at the large place brought her back abruptly to her immediate surroundings; the sound of men shouting, the stamping and whinnying of horses. She stood but could not see anything so she moved forward cautiously. When she reached the first hut she realised that she could see into the building through the wide opening in the side normally closed by a straw blind.

Pleased that the warm weather had given her this opportunity, Medrin kept close and walked along the line of huts, looking into each one. One young woman, standing at the opening to get some air, spotted her and called out.

'I am looking for Borka,' Medrin called back. The woman had lost interest in this poorly dressed person. She gestured to the hut on her left. Putting all thought of caution from her Medrin ran to the door of the hut. It was open and she could see figures moving about inside.

'Borka, is Borka here?' she cried excitedly. There was no answer but after a moment a fat form waddled forward and saw the sad figure of Medrin, shoeless, dirty, and with a shawl round her shoulders even in this heat. She stared unbelievingly. 'Medrin, my lady. What is it?'

'Borka, please. I must speak to you.' She took the woman's arm and almost pulled her out into the open as two more women became interested in what was going on. Borka was protesting, but when they had reached the copse Medrin released her grip.

'My lady, this is very wrong. I . . .'

CHAPTER FIFTEEN

'Listen to me, it is very important,' Medrin interrupted in her most authoritative voice. 'First I must have a good wash and a change of clothes, including good shoes.' She paused, eyeing the woman sternly. 'Then I will tell you something about my uncle Guthrum — a secret which I can tell only you at this time.'

The woman nodded but she seemed uncertain how to take these strange words. Now she noticed the blood on the dress. She pointed a squat and shaking finger at the place. 'Oh, my lady, you have been wounded,' she said, all else forgotten at the sight and its awful implications.

'It is nothing — my horse fell and was killed,' lied Medrin. Her spirits were rising now that her situation seemed to be improving. She went on: 'Do not worry about that — first some clothes and a wash.' As the woman still hesitated. 'You can see to that, can't you?' Her tone was still demanding.

After some grumbling to herself, Borka directed the girl to a stream a few hundred yards away and promised to try and get some clothes. As Medrin made to go: 'Be careful of the stream — men sometimes use it,' she warned. Medrin smiled for the first time in many days and followed a path until she came to the welcome sight of clear, glistening water. She luxuriated in it for some time, forgetting its passing, then made her way back to the huts.

Borka was waiting anxiously and without any change of clothes. 'There is nothing for you here so I will have to take you to my sister,' she explained and later Medrin found herself at a small mud-built dwelling by the shore. She had told Borka that she had an urgent message from Guthrum to rejoin him in England as he was far from well but this information was to be told to no-one, not even her sister Renata. As it happened, the sister was suitably impressed with the rank of her visitor and Borka made it plain to her privately that no questions would be answered.

The two women were both skilled at making and repairing clothing, male and female, so they began to set about preparing a dress for Medrin that would be a great improvement on her present outfit. Borka knew a woman in town who sold remnants and sometimes new clothes; she was able to get a bodice and pieces of skirt. Medrin watched with fascination as the women worked, then Borka had to return to her post at the military centre. Before she left Medrin made another request.

'Borka, one more thing, please. Try and get me a piece of vellum,' she asked again of one who had already put herself in some danger.

'Vellum, Lady Medrin?' the poor woman repeated, not understanding. Tired, with work still to do at the centre, she was beginning to doubt the wisdom of coming to the girl's assistance.

'Yes, please trust me — there is good reason. Any piece will do.'

Grumbling that she did not know where she could be expected to find vellum, Medrin reminded her that she did work at a place where orders would be written and maps made.

The next morning there was no sign of Borka so Renata was sent to find her. She returned within the hour but without Borka — she had made excuses about the amount of work she had to do — or the piece of vellum which she said she was unable to find. In the meantime Medrin had made discreet inquiries at the fish shed about the future departure of ships from the port without naming a destination. She was told that there would be three leaving in two days time. Though she had expected it, the delay irked her but the request to stay a few days longer was accepted by Renata with good grace. Borka came the next day, believing the girl might have left. Asked about the vellum, she shrugged — it was not to be had, she said.

The water in the stream was cool and refreshing for a last bathe. Borka was urged to make a last attempt to find the vellum; now that the time had come when Medrin was going to leave she relented. Up at the house she busied herself but kept looking, and eventually she found a dirty piece under a bed. It appeared to have been used for cleaning footwear and Borka brought it triumphantly, with tears in her eyes, to Medrin. For the first and last time Medrin kissed her and went back to the hut to get a good night's rest before the last stage of her journey.

The ship had raised its sail. Calculating that it would be leaving Haedum within a few minutes, a slender white figure, blonde hair flowing behind her, boarded to the astonishment of the crew.

'Who is your captain?' she snapped at the nearest man. Too surprised for words he pointed amidships to a man giving orders to two others close by. She moved purposefully toward him and waited for him to finish, then announced herself.

'I am Medrin, niece of King Guthrum of East Anglia, and I have orders to join him there.' As the man stroked his bearded chin thoughtfully she handed him the vellum. He took it from her and opened it. It said exactly what she had told him, except that the signature was not original but her copy. She was also relying on the man's inability to read at all. In this she was proved to be right and, after pretending to understand the contents, he nodded and handed the paper back to her. Thus he was saved from embarrassment and her ruse went undiscovered.

As the large Viking ship moved out of the harbour Medrin stood in the bow. It was a beautiful calm day and as she fixed her gaze firmly westward she felt the cool breeze on her face and thought of Athyll. Her instinct told her that he would approve of what she was doing and that with him she would feel more free than ever before. It was this sense of freedom that exhilarated her, a feeling of wellbeing and pride that she had only known once before after her self-imposed winter ordeal at the age of sixteen.

The time went quickly with the ship moving at full speed under sail and ten oarsmen on either side. They had lost sight of the two ships which had followed them out of the harbour as these were fully loaded with stores and had only half the number of oarsmen. Then came darkness and the sudden onset of a strong wind and heavy rain. They struggled on for a time on half sail until the squall increased in intensity; the waves, now twelve feet high, were billowing over the ship, making it difficult for the men to control their oars; they had long since abandoned any attempt to row. Medrin lay full length in the stern where she had been directed as the safest place.

The storm raged on, frequent lightning streaked the air, followed by thunder crashing above, drowning the roar of the waves. The ship was drifting helplessly now, then the lightning struck directly above them. It hit the mast and split it down the middle; it fell, killing one man immediately below and tearing a great gap in the side. Another man was caught by a wave and was swept overboard. As the structure slowly disintegrated parts of it fell away as if a giant hand was tearing it apart, piece by piece. Medrin felt herself being pulled along the bottom and tried desperately to cling to anything that she could grasp. But there was nothing. She found herself being carried forward and tried to stand so as to be able to get a better hold. As she struggled to her feet another wave caught her and she was carried off the ship into the turbulent mass. She tried to swim back to the wreck but the storm was at its height; each attempt to reach out was defeated. She was vaguely conscious of a body floating by and suddenly seized a large plank of wood, then it was swept from under her. Getting weaker now, her breathing became shallower, then, with her last gasp for air she tried to call Athyll's name but no sound came.

THE VIKING GIRL

Some days later a body was washed up on the shore at a bay near the settlement of Lowestoft. It was found by a man and woman walking the beach before the curfew. This was Guthrum's Province and, having seen enough of the consequences of non-co-operation with the Danish forces, they reported immediately to the nearest military camp. The couple were arrested and held for further questioning, then two senior men were sent to inspect their discovery. Unable to identify the body, one of the men recognised the type of footwear which was made in Haedum, which was his home. And from other signs — her height, her features and blonde hair — they deduced she must be one of their own race.

The remains of Medrin were taken to the camp. It was now strongly suspected by those who knew about the King's niece that the body could be hers, so a messenger was sent to Guthrum at his Headquarters at Diss, some forty miles away. Guthrum, on hearing the news, left immediately for the camp.

Looking at the body, though bloated and distorted, the man was in no doubt that this was Medrin. The last time he had seen her she had been strong and well, on her way home; now he was faced by her lifeless body. He stood and cursed the fate which had taken Medrin in this way before she had begun to live in the fullest, most productive sense.

With the local people ordered to stay in their homes, the funeral pyre was prepared at the chosen place where Viking soldiers were taken and honoured with their last rites. Accompanied by Guthrum and a few attendants, Medrin was carried shoulder high and settled on the assembled pile. The king tenderly kissed the girl's forehead, the pyre was lit and gradually she disappeared in the flames.

Chapter 16

When the small party from Southampton arrived back at Winchester Athyll sent Ellen and Harald to the camp to await him there, then went straight to the King. Within an hour of his arrival he was accompanied by Sir Edwig and Aldan and was taken to Alfred.

The King, although preoccupied with many other things at this time, listened patiently as Athyll reported on his visit to the shipyards. Though he had been warned not to take up too much of the King's time, this was unnecessary as he was anxious to keep it brief and to the point. The only interruption came when he mentioned the problem of wood for the ships.

'Oak for pine? Did you satisfy yourself about that?'

'Yes, I think so, sire. I finally had Elfrick's word that it is a good substitute provided that certain conditions are observed.'

'We shall know soon enough if it is not,' muttered Aldan, thinking of the continuing raids on the south coast from the Viking ships. The King was in no mood for comment of this kind, so ignored it. Instead he asked Bowood about manning of the ships. The army commander was caught off guard, but only for a moment.

'I see no problem there,' he said stiffly. Aldan stared fixedly at the wall behind the King's chair, as Alfred waited to hear more. Bowood hesitated, then went on: 'I understand that for some time we have had more people volunteering than we have ships.'

'Sire, can I add to what my lord has said?' asked Athyll.

The King leaned back in his chair. 'Of course — have your say.'

137

'There is a man working on those ships — a man called Wilfred, a sailor and a much experienced man who would be useful and certainly one to be trusted with that task.'

'Very well, then, so he shall be.' He stood and held out his hand to Athyll and Aldan. 'Bowood, I have other affairs to discuss with you, so please stay.'

Athyll left with Aldan, pleased with himself and how he had been needlessly apprehensive about reporting directly to his King. Aldan noticed his self-satisfaction as they walked and slapped him on the shoulder.

'Our King seemed pleased with you,' he said, smiling, but Athyll detected a note of cynicism in the rough voice.

'He had no reason not to be.' His reply was sharp.

Aldan grinned and gave him a more than gentle pat this time. 'Do not get carried away by such things, that's all, lad.'

At the market place Athyll made an excuse that he had to get some purchases and left his companion. When Aldan was out of sight he quickly made his way to Lady Bedford's place. She welcomed him warmly and took him through to the garden which was her favourite place and where she spent a great deal of her time.

'How went your visit to Southampton?' she asked, showing a surprising knowledge of defence information.

'Quite well — very well, thank you,' was all he could say, taken by surprise at the directness of the question. She gestured to a wooden bench and, as he seated himself awkwardly on the edge, she placed herself firmly on a chair opposite.

'Now, why have come to see me?' she asked with that same directness.

Damnation, he thought, this is going to be worse than meeting King Alfred.

'I have a favour to beg of you, my lady,' he said at last. The smile which had been there since she had greeted him quickly faded. But she said nothing and it was her expression which was urging him to continue with his request.

'It is about a serving maid, Ellen.' He paused, watching those unblinking eyes. 'You remember the trial of Egbert for raping the Danish Lady Medrin?'

She nodded. 'Of course.'

'Ellen was the girl who gave evidence for the Dane, my lady, and now she is without work or home.'

CHAPTER SIXTEEN

The stern expression relaxed a little. 'I see. And you wish me to find both for her?' she asked briskly.

'Yes, if it is possible — you will find her honest and a good worker.'

'And what is your interest in this girl, may I ask?'

If Athyll had not had respect for both his questioner and Ellen he would have made apologies and left. However, he did owe the woman a reply.

'She used to work for the camp and had to leave because no payment was being made to the tenant farmer she worked for. I made a promise to help her.' He hesitated, then added lamely: 'She seemed to have become the army's responsibility.'

'But surely not yours, sir.' She rose, went to a particularly fragrant flower and sniffed it appreciatively. 'Very well, bring her to me tomorrow morning and I will see what can be done,' she added, turning her back on the soldier now standing close by. Athyll thanked her and returned to the camp where he found Ellen and told her of his meeting but warned her not to build her hopes up too high.

It happened that Lady Bedford was pleased with the girl and agreed to have her in her household, though she was not strictly in need of another servant. The following weeks were the happiest in Ellen's life. She loved the place where she found herself, and the work, and more important than these, she saw Athyll often. Her cheerfulness, good humour, and love were also good for him; they would go for long walks together and she would surprise him with her knowledge of things related to the countryside. Sometimes she would ride with him on Surgel and they would go further afield — a favourite place was a lake near the forest where they would swim naked, then make love on the verdant growth beside it. Though she was never far from his thoughts, Athyll had decided that Medrin was lost to him from the moment she had boarded the ship for her own country and people.

Then suddenly everything changed. Winchester became a place of tense activity and anxiety, disorganized by urgent movement of men and supplies, when news that a Danish force had left Cambridge and was making its way directly to the southwest. There had also been rumours of a fleet moving directly up the Channel from the west, probably Ireland, and there were fears that there was a connection between the two movements. King Alfred immediately went to Cheddar with his retinue and military commanders and set up his headquarters there so as to stop the Danish advance to the coast.

Two days later his forces met up with the Danes who had moved quickly. The ensuing battle was nearly a total disaster for the Saxons. With a force which was inferior in numbers, the Danes were able to take them by surprise before they could deploy their forces. Coming among the Saxons suddenly they caused heavy casualties and many fled in panic to give themselves up later as hostages. But the Danes, not knowing that Alfred was with his troops, retired satisfied and the King, accompanied now by a much smaller force, fell back inside the more secure perimeter of his kingdom west of Selwood Forest, which marked the boundary between the bishoprics of Winchester and Sherbourne.

From the protection of the forest, where his force remained and was strengthened from time to time, Alfred moved out some months later to build a fortress at Athelney on the Somerset marshes and from here he carried out a series of harassing raids against the Danes in preparation for the full-scale attack when he considered that time had come.

In the Spring he was strong enough to move to the eastern side of Selwood, where his Somerset men joined forces with others from the southern counties. Reaching Edington, south of Chippenham, his advance troops located the enemy and Alfred made plans for the attack, which he intended to be so strong and devastating that the Danes would be in final retreat from his kingdom to those parts of the country where they were so entrenched that he was prepared to let them stay until the unification of the whole of England, which was his ultimate goal. Though Alfred doubted that he would live to see that time, he was now dedicated to those first steps which had to be taken before the cherished result could be achieved.

Some eight thousand men — with two thousand of these in reserve — were lined up facing the Danes to the west. They were formed in a semicircle; to the left and right were serried rows of archers, behind them men with spears, clubs and catapults, at the rear were most of the cavalry, protecting the King and his retinue in the centre but also ready to give support to those in front of them.

Patrols which had gone ahead of the main body reported that the Danes appeared to be only partly prepared; some archers with bows ready were alert and there were mounted men moving about, but generally there seemed an arrogant contempt for any danger. So came the order to attack. The plan was to take the Danes by surprise, to draw them out and to completely encircle them so that they would have no way to escape and either surrender or be destroyed.

Now the whole Saxon army moved slowly forward to high ground. Once there the archers went into action and arrows fell with deadly effect into the Danish camp. There were casualties and confusion for a while but as more arrows rained down the enemy rallied quickly and their archers responded, running as they did so. Athyll, with the troops on the left flank, went amongst them, preparing them for the counter-attack. At the top of the high ground he could see Saxon men running toward the Danes, then joining them in fierce hand-to-hand fighting. The order had been to hold the high ground at all cost but there was nothing he could do about those who ignored it; he sat watching, then noticed Black Edward among a group of Danes who were attacking him. He seemed to have lost his bow but was swinging his great arms about him to some effect when he was taken from behind by a man with a club. Over to Athyll's right he could see that some Danes had broken through the first rank of archers.

It was difficult for him to see what was actually happening; as he stood in the saddle to get a better view a horseman came pounding towards him and as he approached he waved and shouted to all group commanders: 'Get your men forward.' Athyll was soon joined by four other cavalrymen and, yelling to the rest of the men, they swept down the hill right into the middle of a group of Danes. Athyll put one down with his sword and as the others laid about them there soon was a pile of bodies left on the ground. Followed by those on foot screaming for victims, they carried on to chase those now in retreat.

As the battle went on unabated in fury and ruthlessness, it was clear that the Danes were suffering great casualties and were fighting desperately for survival. Athyll, tired and choked with dust, rode from one Saxon group to another, the cavalry continuing to give individual assistance where it was needed before being called on to fight as one body in that final attack. He had helped to save Harald, who had been wounded, and now noticed that several of the enemy had broken away from a band of Saxon soldiers who had been savagely trying to hack or club them to death or submission.

Reaching them he swung his bloodstained and blunted sword at the nearest Dane, a very tall, muscular man wielding an axe. As the sword came down on him he moved with surprising speed, parrying it with his axe, and at the same time he caught the Saxon's free arm. There was a brief struggle until the big man's superior strength told against Athyll and he was pulled from the saddle, landing at his enemy's feet. He lifted the axe arm high and made to bring it down when Surgel reared and brought his front hooves down with terrible force on the Dane's bare chest, drawing blood from a gaping wound. He fell back and Athyll, now on his feet, plunged his sword into the place. It snapped off as he did so and he threw it away with a scream of rage. He turned to Surgel, now sweating and trembling, and went to remount. As he did so he sensed rather than saw somebody behind him and turned to face him.

A man who had seen his fellow Dane killed had come running up and Athyll saw him lifting his club but it had happened so quickly he was unable to move out of the way. It crashed down on his head; his helmet took part of the blow, there was a searing pain above his eyes. As he fell a roaring sound deafened him, the sky blurred, became darker and darker; and he was not conscious of the large Saxon face which then appeared, destroying his attacker and overcoming those remaining Danes who had not been able to escape.

Sometime later, as the sun was setting, what remained of the Viking force surrendered; it was a total victory for King Alfred and his army. But, exhausted and reduced in numbers, they watched in silence as Guthrum slowly rode up to the King and handed him his sword. With equal dignity Alfred passed the sword to Bowood, reached out and took the Dane's hand in a firm grip. The courteous acknowledgement of his enemy's surrender was brief. The King turned to Bowood: 'To Athelney,' he called.

Then, at Aller, close to the stronghold, Guthrum and thirty of his army's leaders were received by Alfred and Guthrum was baptized a Christian. He made it clear to the King that this was not due to his defeat at Edington but would not give his reasons for having changed his pagan beliefs, after having held them for a lifetime. Now a treaty was made; Guthrum undertook to leave Wessex, never to return, and led his army first to Gloucester, then finally back to East Anglia.

Athyll awoke, opened his eyes and was conscious of severe pain. All was dark; he thought it must be night and wondered where he was. His mind was unclear and as he tried to collect his thoughts the moments before he lost all knowledge of time and place gradually came to him. He cried out as he relived the blow that had felled him and the confusion of sounds that had accompanied it; a horse whinnying, a man screaming, and that last dreadful roar of noise in his ears. Now it was delirium and he kept asking for Medrin, time and time again he called her name. It was another twenty-four hours before he recovered.

He found his vision not yet focused on anything but he could feel his back and legs chaffing against something rough and reached out behind him. He was laying on a bed of straw matting and tried to get up. The effort was too much for him and he fell back. Voices were heard clearly now and he realised he was not alone. He called out for help, weakly at first, then he managed a desperate shout. He waited. There was sound of movement, of heavy footsteps coming toward him. A strong hand touched his arm.

'Who is that?' The shouted question sounded panic-stricken.

'Sir, it is me, Harald.'

Athyll tried to sit up and this time he was helped. As he was made more comfortable, with his back resting on a wall behind him, he said, more quietly now; 'Where in God's name am I?'

'You were brought down in the battle, sir.'

'That tells me nothing I do not know,' Athyll said sharply.

'Yes, but all of us here are wounded — we be waiting to go back to Winchester.'

Athyll stared hard, trying to place the man. He was also conscious of the stench of putrifying flesh. 'It is so dark in here — for heaven's sake, can you not open a door?'

There was silence. 'Harald, are you still there?' The panic in his voice had returned as the truth was slowly dawning on him.

'Yes, sir. I am here. The doors are both open.'

The wounded who had survived were removed as quickly as possible from that place near Cheddar where they had been taken from the battlefield. Harald had fortunately recovered in a short time from the gash in his side inflicted by a spear and he made it his business to go to Lady Bedford's home and seek out Ellen. As a member of the Anglo-Saxon army which had just defeated the Danes, he had no qualms about going directly to the place and almost demanding to see Lady Bedford herself.

The tall woman who saw him, almost as imposing as her mistress, demurred anxiously as the young soldier made his request.

'You say the matter is urgent. Before I can see my lady I have to know why.'

Harald shuffled a little in embarrassment. 'I would like to tell the Lady Bedford myself.' He added, as an after-thought. 'It is not about me — it is about an officer, Athyll of York.'

The woman considered for a moment. 'I am sorry but that is not good enough — you must tell me more.'

At this point Lady Bedford appeared. She saw the two, went to them with an admonishment ready for what seemed to be an unwelcomed intrusion. Then she saw the soldier and her attitude changed.

'This man is demanding to see you, my lady . . .' began the woman but was stopped in mid-sentence.

'Then I will deal with it, Gertrude. You may go.'

The woman curtsied slowly and left with the same lack of haste. Lady Bedford allowed a smile to linger for a moment and turned to Harald.

'Now, young man, I hope you are not going to waste my time,' she told him, not unkindly.

'No, my lady, I will not — it is very important.' Then it came out in a rush; how Athyll had been seriously wounded in the head, though his horse Surgel was safe; how he thought that Ellen should know and be allowed to see him. 'With your permission, my lady,' he concluded, watching anxiously for her reaction. She reached out and touched his arm. He was surprised to see tears in her eyes.

'That will be arranged, you have my word for it.' She paused. 'There is more than one reason why I think it very necessary,' she added, but more to herself than her listener.

No time was lost; Lady Bedford arranged for Athyll to be brought to the house without delay. His fractured skull was healing well but he was still very weak and he was settled in a room which had been Bedford's. After he had been there some days he received a visit from Sir Edwig and Aldan, who had been knighted after the battle of Edington. Sir Edwig came straight to the point. The King was going to grant him sixty acres of land to do as he wished, he told Athyll. 'You can choose whichever place you like and you will have no difficulty in getting labour to help you,' he added.

'Yes, we will be losing a lot of men now,' put in Sir Aldan gloomily. 'Strange how victory can bring as many problems as it solves.' Then, after a brief silence, they told him of Medrin's death.

Athyll expressed his gratitude for the King's consideration and their news but said little more; he was in no mood for talk. Noting how he must be feeling, they cut short their visit and left him with their hope for his continued recovery, since no one could say how long his blindness would last.

CHAPTER SIXTEEN

The following day Lady Bedford sent for Ellen. Quite happy in her ladyship's service and usually at ease in her presence, the girl was nevertheless made nervous these days by any sudden call to see her. She had seen Athyll only once since he had arrived; the memory of how she had stood uncertainly beside his bed, and that he had known it was she without seeing her, had sustained her all the long days since. Now she feared there might be something wrong. She walked slowly to the bedchamber, anxiously wondering what she was going to hear. She entered and was told to take a seat, an unusual request.

'Is it Athyll?' she asked nervously. 'Is he worse?'

Lady Bedford gave one of her rare smiles. 'No, of course not. In fact he is quite well and has asked to see you.' Ellen leaned forward eagerly and was about to speak. A hand was held to stop her.

'Now, go to him, Ellen, and tell him about the child. I think he will want to marry you but, remember, we women must retain our dignity at all costs, must we not?' She smiled again.

Ellen nodded, also smiling, but not fully understanding. Lady Bedford led her to the door and watched as she started to run, then stop and clutch her stomach. Now she continued, walking as fast as she could. She reached his room and almost fell as she rushed to his bed. Ellen paused there, looking at him, uncertain of herself. He called out: 'Ellen, is that you?'

She kissed him. 'Yes, it is me — it is me.' Suddenly she stood back, near to tears, grateful that he could not see them when they came.

'Athyll, I have something to tell you,' she said softly.

He turned in the direction of the voice. 'I think I know.' He reached out for her hand. 'I have been given sixty acres by the King — I want a son to help me.'

'Yes, Athyll — we both will,' she told him.

He lay back on the bed in a moment of pain and anguish which he hoped went unnoticed by Ellen. With Medrin dead his hope of seeing her again, being with her, now shattered he knew that, for good or ill — who could tell — his life, from this moment on, would be bound to Ellen and his child, and his acres of land, wherever they might be.